BAYSIDE BEGINNINGS

MAGNOLIA KEY

BOOK FIVE

KAY CORRELL

ZURA LU PUBLISHING LLC

Published by Zura Lu Publishing LLC

Some secrets refuse to stay buried, even in paradise.

Felicity Bond thought she was retreating for a quiet summer at her grandmother's cozy bed and breakfast, but the island has other plans. Instead, she finds herself helping charming historian Brent Dunn unravel an island mystery involving a visiting prince, a forbidden romance, and a scandal that's haunted the local families for generations.

But as they delve deeper into the past, they discover that some secrets are best left buried. Felicity must decide whether to follow her heart or play it safe, even as Brent's own family history becomes entangled in the mystery.

In this heartwarming tale of new beginnings, second chances, and the enduring power of love, Felicity learns that Magnolia Key has a way of revealing what each person needs most—if only they're brave enough to accept it. Filled with richly drawn characters, emotional depth, and the singular charm of the Florida coast, this enchanting story explores the joy of finding your true path and the courage to pursue it.

The Wedding in the Grove - (a crossover short story between series - with Josephine and Paul from The Letter.)

LIGHTHOUSE POINT ~ THE SERIES
Wish Upon a Shell - Book One
Wedding on the Beach - Book Two
Love at the Lighthouse - Book Three
Cottage near the Point - Book Four
Return to the Island - Book Five
Bungalow by the Bay - Book Six
Christmas Comes to Lighthouse Point - Book Seven

CHARMING INN ~ Return to Lighthouse Point
One Simple Wish - Book One
Two of a Kind - Book Two
Three Little Things - Book Three
Four Short Weeks - Book Four
Five Years or So - Book Five
Six Hours Away - Book Six
Charming Christmas - Book Seven

SWEET RIVER ~ THE SERIES
A Dream to Believe in - Book One
A Memory to Cherish - Book Two

A Song to Remember - Book Three
A Time to Forgive - Book Four
A Summer of Secrets - Book Five
A Moment in the Moonlight - Book Six

MOONBEAM BAY ~ THE SERIES

The Parker Women - Book One
The Parker Cafe - Book Two
A Heather Parker Original - Book Three
The Parker Family Secret - Book Four
Grace Parker's Peach Pie - Book Five
The Perks of Being a Parker - Book Six

BLUE HERON COTTAGES ~ THE SERIES

Memories of the Beach - Book One
Walks along the Shore - Book Two
Bookshop near the Coast - Book Three
Restaurant on the Wharf - Book Four
Lilacs by the Sea - Book Five
Flower Shop on Magnolia - Book Six
Christmas by the Bay - Book Seven
Sea Glass from the Past - Book Eight

MAGNOLIA KEY ~ THE SERIES

Saltwater Sunrise - Book One
Encore Echoes - Book Two

Coastal Candlelight - Book Three
Tidal Treasures - Book Four
Bayside Beginnings - Book Five
And more to come!

CHRISTMAS SEASHELLS AND SNOWFLAKES
Seaside Christmas Wishes

WIND CHIME BEACH ~ A stand-alone novel

INDIGO BAY ~
Sweet Days by the Bay - Kay's Complete Collection of stories in the Indigo Bay series

Sign up for my newsletter at my website *kaycorrell.com* to make sure you don't miss any new releases or sales.

CHAPTER 1

Felicity glanced around the classroom, checking to make sure she'd gotten everything off the walls. Her students' desks were scooted to the center of the room with the chairs piled on top of them. Two boxes sat on her desk, filled with her personal items. No school-day chaos rang through the hallways. The students were gone for the summer, and the only sound in her classroom was the faint tick of the clock.

She picked up one box and settled it on her hip. Hard to believe a school year was wrapped up in just two boxes. Her summer break was the time when she could relax and rejuvenate. Her salvation from a long, hard year. Only this time, she didn't think a summer was enough time to recover.

The air, normally thick with the scent of chalk dust and old textbooks, felt strangely sterile, a twin to the emptiness that had taken root inside of her. Each year, packing up her classroom usually brought a sense of relief, the promise of lazy days and time to recharge. This year, it felt more like closing the door on a chapter she wasn't sure she wanted to revisit.

The weight of another year's worth of expectations and unfulfilled potential pressed down on her, heavy and suffocating. The walls, usually plastered with colorful charts and student artwork, now stood bare, exposing drab beige paint beneath. Even the afternoon sunlight seemed to hesitate at the window, as if reluctant to peek in on the forlorn scene.

As Felicity turned to lift the second box, she caught a glimpse of a small, forgotten photograph tucked behind the corner of her desk. It was a picture of her very first class, their smiles wide and genuine, capturing a moment when teaching felt like magic. She gently plucked the photo from its hiding place, dusting off the edges. The faces stared back at her, reminding her of a time when every day brought new discoveries and her heart was full of hope. She remembered the vibrant energy of those early days, the laughter, the shared triumphs of discovering something new. The pure joy of learning.

The room felt empty, but not just of people —empty of the warmth and exuberance that once filled it. She placed the photo carefully in the box, a small memento of a time when teaching was a calling, not just a day-to-day job to get through.

Felicity glanced one last time around the classroom, her eyes lingering on the spaces where she'd taped up her students' best work, the places that had once been filled with color and life. The room seemed to sigh with her as if bidding her a silent farewell. She turned off the lights, the switch clicking definitively under her fingers, and stepped out into the hallway. The door closed behind her with a finality she wasn't quite ready to face.

With a deep breath, she adjusted the boxes in her arms and made her way down the familiar corridor. The echo of her footsteps seemed to resonate with the memories that clung to every corner of the school. Each step carried the weight of years spent molding young minds, the highs and lows of a career that had once defined her.

She pushed open the heavy doors leading outside, and the humid summer air wrapped around her. The scent of freshly cut grass and the distant laughter of children playing filled the air. The world outside the school was alive, teeming with the promise of a new season—and endless summer. She squinted against the bright sunlight, letting it warm her face as she walked to her car.

She loaded the boxes into the trunk, a feeling of finality settling over her. The school year was over, and with it, a chapter of her life seemed to be drawing to a close. She slid into the driver's seat and started the engine, the familiar purr of her old sedan soothing her jangled nerves.

As she pulled out of the parking lot, the school building receded in her rearview mirror. Tomorrow she'd be at Gran's place on Magnolia Key. An island that had always been her salvation. A place to rest and recharge. Only this time, she wasn't sure a summer would be long enough.

Felicity stepped off the ferry, her sandals hitting the sun-warmed wood of the dock as the familiar scent of salt air and blooming magnolias embraced her. Instantly some of the tension in her shoulders eased. Magnolia Key always had that effect on her—like coming home to a warm hug.

She scanned the small crowd gathered near the ferry landing, searching for Gran's familiar face. A smile tugged at her lips as she spotted her waving enthusiastically from beside her ancient station wagon.

"Felicity! Over here, sweetheart!" Gran called out, her voice carrying easily over the chatter of tourists and locals.

She waved back and made her way through the throng, pulling her wheeled suitcase behind her. As soon as she was within reach, Gran wrapped her in a tight hug that smelled of lavender and fresh-baked cookies.

"Oh, it's so good to see you," Gran said, holding Felicity at arm's length to look her over. "You look tired, dear. Was the trip okay?"

She nodded, feeling a lump form in her throat at her grandmother's concern. "The trip was fine, Gran. It's just been a long year."

Gran's eyes softened with understanding.

"Well, you're here now. We'll get you settled and rested in no time." She patted Felicity's shoulder affectionately before turning to open the car door.

As they drove through town, Felicity gazed out the window, drinking in the familiar sights. Not much had changed since her last visit— the same quaint storefronts lined Main Street, their awnings fluttering in the sea breeze. The old gazebo in the town square still stood proudly, its white paint gleaming in the afternoon sun.

Beverly, the owner of Coastal Coffee, was standing outside the cafe and waved to them as they approached. Gran slowed down, and Beverly poked her head in the window. "Felicity, glad to see you. Afternoon, Darlene. Felicity, your grandmother has been looking forward to your visit this summer."

"Hi, Beverly. I've been looking forward to coming here too."

"Make sure you stop by and have a meal or two at the cafe. We'll catch up."

"I'll do that," she assured Beverly.

"I can't tell you how glad I am to have you here for the summer," Gran said as she pulled away and navigated down the winding coastal road toward the bay. "The summer booking calendar is fuller than ever this year."

She turned from the window. "I'm happy to help out however I can, Gran. That's why I'm here."

Gran glanced at her, a knowing look on her face. "Now, don't you go worrying about work just yet. I want you to take some time to relax first. Heaven knows you need it after a year of wrangling all those kids."

"But Gran, I—"

"No buts," Gran interrupted, her tone gentle but firm. "The B&B has been running just fine without you so far. A few more days won't hurt. I want you to take at least a week to unwind before you even think about helping out."

Felicity opened her mouth to protest, then thought better of it. She knew that look in her grandmother's eyes. There was no point in arguing.

"All right, Gran," she conceded with a small smile. "A week of relaxation it is."

Gran nodded, satisfied. "Good. Now, tell me all about your year. How were your students this time around?"

As she began to recount tales from her

classroom, she felt some of the heaviness lift from her heart. Maybe Gran was right. Maybe what she needed most right now was time—to rest, to think, to rediscover the joy that had led her to teaching in the first place.

As the car turned onto the familiar crushed shell drive of Bayside Bed and Breakfast, the old Victorian house came into view. Its weathered shingles and wraparound porch were as inviting as ever.

She followed Gran into Bayside B&B, the familiar creak of the front door a welcome sound after her long trip. Her long year.

The entryway was awash in warm sunlight that streamed through the sparkling clean windows and splashed across the polished hardwood floors. The faint scent of yeasty bread and cinnamon greeted her. The cheerful atmosphere seemed at odds with the bone-deep weariness she felt.

"Home sweet home," Gran said, setting Felicity's suitcase down. "Let's get you settled in."

She nodded, too tired to muster much enthusiasm. She trailed after Gran up the stairs, her feet heavy on each step. Framed photographs of the island—vibrant sunsets, pristine beaches, and lush gardens—lined the wall. She remembered how those images used to fill her with excitement and anticipation. Now, they only served to highlight how drained she felt.

"I've put you in room seven," Gran said as they reached the second-floor landing. "I know it's always been your favorite. You have that nice window seat with a view of the bay."

A small spark of warmth kindled in her. "Thanks, Gran. That's really thoughtful of you. I love that room." How many hours had she sat on that window seat, looking out over the water? Watching the sunrise? Watching the ferry cross the bay?

Gran led the way down the hall, her floral skirt swishing with each step. She unlocked the door to room seven and swung it open with a flourish. "Here we are! I freshened it up just this morning."

She stepped inside and was immediately wrapped in the room's familiar comfort. The afternoon sun poured through the bay windows, illuminating the soft butter-yellow walls and making the white eyelet curtains glow. The antique four-poster bed was neatly made with a patchwork quilt she recognized from her childhood visits.

"Oh, Gran," she breathed, some of her fatigue lifting. "It's perfect."

Gran beamed, clearly pleased. "I'm so glad you like it. Now, why don't you get settled in and rest for a bit? I'll bring you up some iced tea and snacks later."

She nodded gratefully. "That sounds wonderful. Thank you."

Once Gran had bustled out of the room, gently closing the door behind her, Felicity sank onto the bed with a heavy sigh. She kicked off her sandals and lay back, letting the soft mattress cradle her tired body. The ceiling fan spun lazily overhead, its gentle whir a soothing white noise.

She turned her head to gaze out the window. From this vantage point, she could see a slice of the sparkling bay beyond the lush green of Gran's garden. A light breeze carried the scent of salt and blooming flowers through the open window.

Everything about the island seemed so alive, so vibrant. The blunt contrast to her own state of exhaustion filled her with an emotion she couldn't quite name. She closed her eyes, hoping a nap might bridge the gap between her inner weariness and the sunny paradise outside.

CHAPTER 2

The next morning, Felicity woke to sunlight streaming through the eyelet curtains. She blinked, momentarily disoriented, before remembering where she was. Magnolia Key. Gran's B&B. An entire summer stretching out before her.

She sat up, surprised to find that she felt more rested than she had in months. The weight of the school year seemed to have lifted slightly, replaced by the gentle island breeze drifting through her open window. That was the nice thing about being right on the water—the breeze often chased the normal coastal humidity away.

After a quick shower, she made her way downstairs, following the irresistible aroma of coffee and bacon. In the kitchen, she found Gran bustling about, flipping pancakes and humming softly to herself.

"Good morning, sleepyhead," Gran said with a warm smile. "I was beginning to think you'd sleep the day away."

She glanced at the clock, surprised to see it was nearly nine. "I guess I needed the rest more than I realized," she admitted, settling onto a stool at the kitchen island.

Gran set a steaming mug of coffee in front of her. "That's what summer break is for, isn't it? Now, how about some breakfast?"

Before she could answer, a plate piled high with fluffy pancakes, crisp bacon, and fresh strawberries appeared before her. The sight and smell made her stomach growl appreciatively.

As she ate, she watched Gran move efficiently around the kitchen, preparing breakfast for the B&B guests. She felt a twinge of guilt for not helping, but Gran waved away her offers of assistance.

"You just enjoy your breakfast," Gran insisted. "There'll be plenty of time for you to help out later."

She nodded, enjoying each bite of her meal. When she finished, she insisted on at least washing her own dishes, ignoring Gran's protests.

After breakfast, she wandered into the main part of the B&B, taking in the familiar sights and sounds. The old grandfather clock in the corner ticked steadily, its face gleaming in the morning light. Colorful throw pillows adorned the comfortable sofas in the sitting room, inviting guests to relax and unwind.

Her attention was drawn to a large bulletin board near the front desk. It was covered with flyers and notices, a colorful collage of island life. She read through the various announcements—a farmers' market on Saturdays, yoga classes on the beach, a local art show. Oh, and there it was, Gran's weekly knitting group. She smiled as she remembered Gran trying to teach her to knit. Her stitches had never looked as nice and even as Gran's, but she'd enjoyed the time sitting and chatting with Gran's knitting friends. They'd always been so nice to her and included her as one of their own.

One flyer in particular caught her eye. It advertised a talk by Brent Dunn in a few weeks at the community center about the history of southern Florida. She found herself intrigued.

She'd always been interested in history, and learning more about the area seemed like a perfect way to ease into her summer on the island.

She made a mental note of the date and time, thinking it might be a nice outing. As she turned away from the bulletin board, a spark of curiosity and anticipation flickered through her —emotions she hadn't experienced in far too long.

Brent Dunn leaned against the railing of the ferry, his eyes fixed on the shoreline of Magnolia Key as it grew larger. The gentle breeze tousled his hair, carrying with it the salty scent of the sea. He inhaled deeply, allowing the anticipation of his upcoming project to wash over him.

As a historian specializing in the early development of Florida, he had chosen this small island as the perfect base for his latest research project. Its quieter pace and rich local lore made it an ideal location to jump into his work without the distractions of the mainland.

The ferry's horn sounded, signaling their imminent arrival. He made his way back to his car and joined the line of vehicles waiting to disembark. He drummed his fingers on the steering wheel, his mind already racing with ideas and lists of to-dos.

The ferry's engines rumbled to a halt as it gently eased up to the dock with a soft thud. As the cars began to roll off, he steered his car in line. Once on solid ground, he pulled out his phone and entered the address for the Bayside Bed and Breakfast. He'd chosen the place for its central location and the promise of a quiet, comfortable base for his work. As he followed the GPS directions, he took in the charming scenery of the island—quaint shops, colorful houses in shades of sea foam and coral, and glimpses of sparkling turquoise water between the buildings.

As he navigated the narrow, winding roads, the scenery gradually shifted. Soon, he pulled into a tidy parking lot adjacent to a lovely two-story house that looked like it had stepped out of a postcard. A wooden sign, its paint slightly faded by sun and salt air, proclaimed "Bayside B&B" in swooping letters. He eased his car into a spot, cut the engine, and stepped out. He arched his back, working out the kinks from the drive, and breathed in deeply. This was exactly the change of pace he needed.

He took a moment to appreciate the building's wraparound porch and the cheerful flower boxes adorning the windows. The place exuded a welcoming warmth that made him feel instantly at ease. He grabbed his computer from the front seat and retrieved his luggage from the trunk, his mind already shifting gears to the work ahead. He climbed the steps to the porch, eager to start his work.

Felicity stepped into the foyer just as a man entered, carrying his luggage. She recognized the familiar rhythm of a new guest arriving and instinctively moved to assist him, falling into the routine she'd learned from helping Gran over the years.

"Welcome to Bayside Bed and Breakfast," she said, giving him a warm, welcoming smile. "I'm Felicity. Darlene Bond, the owner, is my grandmother. Let me help you get settled in."

The man returned her smile. "Thank you, Felicity. I'm Brent Dunn. It's a pleasure to meet you."

As she led him to the front desk, she glanced at the reservation book, noting that Gran had assigned him to room five, right next to her own room. She picked up the key and gestured for Brent to follow her up the stairs.

"So, what brings you to Magnolia Key, Mr. Dunn?" she asked as they climbed the steps, the old wooden floorboards creaking beneath their feet.

"Please, call me Brent," he said, his voice warm and friendly. "I'm a historian, and I'm here to research the early development of southern Florida. Magnolia Key seemed like the perfect place to start."

"Oh, I saw on Gran's bulletin board of activities that you're giving a talk later this month."

"I am."

"I've already made a note of the date and time. I'm planning to attend. And I'm sure you'll find plenty of interesting stories and history here on the island during your stay."

They reached the second floor, and she led him down the hallway to room five. She unlocked the door and stepped aside, allowing him to enter first.

"Here you are, Brent. If you need anything

at all during your stay, please don't hesitate to ask. Gran and I are always happy to help."

Brent set his luggage down and turned to face her. "You have Wi-Fi, right?"

"We do. The password is written on the welcome packet on the desk in the corner. Breakfast is each morning from seven to nine or so. And There's a list of restaurants on the island in the packet too. Most places are walkable."

"Thank you."

"I'll leave you to settle in." She pulled the door behind her and went to tell Gran she'd checked in a guest.

She found Gran in the kitchen, busy baking pie crusts for quiche for tomorrow's breakfast. "Gran, I checked in Mr. Dunn. He's the man giving the talk on the history of the area later this month."

Gran turned and looked at her, shaking her head. "And that's how you relax and take some time off?"

She grinned. "Pretty much."

She leaned against the kitchen counter, watching as Gran rolled out another pie crust with practiced ease. The familiar scent of butter and flour filled the air, bringing back memories of childhood summers spent in this very kitchen.

"Anyway, I just wanted to help out," she said. "It's why I'm here, after all. I can't take up a prime guest room and not earn my keep."

Gran paused and turned to face her, wiping her flour-covered hands on her apron. "Sweetheart, you're here to rest and recharge. I appreciate your help, but you've only just arrived. There's plenty of time for you to pitch in later."

Maybe Gran was right, but the idea of sitting idle made her uncomfortable. "I know, but I feel better when I'm doing something productive."

"I get it, honey. But sometimes the most productive thing you can do is take care of yourself. Why don't you go for a walk on the beach? The weather's perfect for it."

She glanced out the window. The sun was shining brightly and it did look inviting. "I suppose a little fresh air wouldn't hurt," she admitted reluctantly.

Gran smiled. "That's the spirit. Go on, enjoy the sunshine."

She hesitated for a moment, then nodded.

"All right, Gran. I'll go for a walk. But promise you'll let me help with breakfast tomorrow?"

"Deal," Gran said with a wink. "Now scoot. I want to see some sand between your toes when you get back."

With a small laugh, Felicity headed for the door. As she stepped outside, the warm island breeze caressed her face, and she felt a tiny knot of tension in her shoulders begin to unravel. Maybe Gran was right.

Wasn't she always right?

Maybe what she needed most right now was simply to breathe.

CHAPTER 3

Felicity woke early the next morning to the gentle sound of waves on the shore. Despite Gran's insistence that she take it easy, she quickly got dressed, eager to help with breakfast preparations.

"I told you to rest," Gran said, shaking her head as Felicity entered the kitchen.

"I am rested," she insisted, tying an apron around her waist. "Besides, I promised I'd help with breakfast, remember?"

Gran sighed but relented, handing her a bowl of muffin batter. "All right, I guess There's no use standing here arguing with you."

They worked side by side, the familiar routine of preparing breakfast for the guests bringing her a feeling of purpose. As she stirred the batter and poured it into the muffin tins, she found her mind drifting away from the stress and uncertainty that had plagued her in recent months.

The guests trickled in, filling the dining room with quiet chatter and the clinking of dishes. She moved between the kitchen and dining room, refilling coffee cups and ensuring everyone had what they needed, a routine she easily fell into after years of helping Gran when she came to visit.

As the morning wore on, the guests gradually departed until only Brent remained, nursing a cup of coffee and poring over some papers spread out on the table.

He looked up from his papers when she came in with the coffeepot to refill his mug. "Would you like to take a break and join me?"

She glanced back toward the kitchen. "I guess I could for a few minutes. Then I want to help Gran finish cleaning up the kitchen."

She grabbed a cup of coffee and sank into the chair. "How's the research coming along?"

"Fascinating, actually," he replied, his eyes lighting up. "I've uncovered some intriguing details about the early settlers of Magnolia Key. Did you know that—"

"Now, now," Gran interrupted, bustling into the room with a plate of muffins. "Don't go spoiling all your stories before your talk, Mr. Dunn. We want to leave some surprises for the audience."

Brent laughed. "You're right, of course. My apologies."

Gran set the plate down on the table. "Fresh from the oven. Help yourselves."

Brent reached for one. "I thought I was full after that delicious quiche, but I can't pass up these muffins."

"Gran, sit and join us. Then I'll help you clean up."

"I could do that." Gran got a cup of coffee, sat down, and looked over at Brent, nodding toward the papers spread beside him. "So, what made you decide to come to Magnolia Key for your research?"

"The island has a rich history. All the areas around here do. I want to go over to Belle Island for some research and also to the Moonbeam Bay area."

"All lovely places." Gran nodded.

"I'm looking forward to exploring all of them."

"Well, obviously, Magnolia Key is my

favorite," Gran said. "And you know, Magnolia Key is special. It has a way of revealing what people are searching for, even if they don't know they're looking."

"What do you mean, Gran?"

Gran smiled cryptically. "Oh, just that this island has a bit of magic to it. People come here for all sorts of reasons, but they often leave with something they didn't expect to find."

"Like what?" Brent asked, leaning forward with interest.

"Could be anything," Gran replied. "A new perspective, a forgotten passion, maybe even…" She trailed off, her eyes twinkling. "Well, who knows? That's the beauty of it. You never know what you might discover about yourself here on Magnolia Key."

Felicity helped Gran clean up the kitchen, then offered to help with more work that needed to be done. "Don't argue with me, Gran. I'm here to help. I like helping. What can I do?"

"I've been meaning to hang up some white twinkle lights on the porch railing. Don't you think that would look nice? Just add a nice ambiance in the evenings for guests who like to sit out on the porch and look out over the bay."

"I think that's a great idea."

"I'm pretty sure I have some in the storage shed, but I haven't had time to go look and check."

"I can look for them."

"Great, then I'll get started on some dough for cinnamon rolls for tomorrow."

Felicity walked outside and cut across the yard to the shed. Gran called it a shed, but it was actually a cute little structure with a gabled roof, white shutters, and a small porch of its own. As a young girl, she'd made herself a small area inside with a little table and chair and called it her very own house. She smiled at the thought.

She opened the door and stepped inside. Shelves lined both sides of the small space, filled with Christmas decorations, old board games, painting supplies, extra linens, and everything else that didn't fit inside the bed and breakfast. She scanned the shelves, looking for the lights. When she spotted a box labeled "twinkle lights" on a high shelf, she pulled over a step stool and climbed up to reach it.

After pulling it off the shelf, she balanced it

on her hip as she climbed down again. There was still a stack of books on the table in the special area she'd had as a young girl. Not much changed around here.

She set the box of twinkle lights on the table beside the books and turned back to the shelves. She'd loved looking through the boxes when she was younger, and it appeared that she hadn't changed much. She popped open the lid of a box near her and peered inside. A stack of leather books rested inside. She pulled the top one out and opened it. It was an old guest register.

She frowned. Gran had owned the bed and breakfast for years. Felicity hadn't realized it had been one even before that. She remembered Gran had done some renovations on the building to make it so each room had its own bathroom and create a couple of suites in the building. She must have been something like seven or eight when Gran made those improvements.

She walked outside with the box and sat down, slowly looking through the guest book. So many names over so many years. She dug down into the box and pulled out the bottom book. Surprise crept through her when she realized how old it was. Some of the entries were dated back to the early 1900s.

She jumped as a shadow fell across the book in her hands. She looked up, meeting Brent's curious gaze. How long had he been standing there?

"Oh, you startled me," she said, hoping her voice didn't betray the sudden rapid beating of her heart. She tucked a loose strand of hair behind her ear, buying herself a moment to regain composure.

"I'm sorry. I didn't mean to scare you." He gestured toward the book. "What have you got there? It looks pretty old."

She held up the leather-bound volume, angling it so he could see the faded lettering on the spine. "It's an old guest book. From before Gran owned Bayside. I found it when I was looking for twinkle lights."

He came closer and peered at the book with interest. "Fascinating. May I?"

She handed it to him. "Some of the entries are very old. I had no idea this building was an inn that far back."

Brent carefully flipped through the brittle pages, his brow creasing in concentration. "Do you mind if I take a closer look at this?" he asked, his gaze still fixed on the faded script.

"I'm sure Gran wouldn't mind." She stood, tucking the other guest books back into the box. "Let's go ask her."

They found Gran was in the kitchen, her hands covered in flour as she kneaded dough.

"Gran, we found some old guest books in the shed," she said. "Brent was hoping to take a closer look at them. Would that be all right?"

"Guest books?" Gran wiped her hands on her apron. "Now, wouldn't that be a peek into the past?" She turned to Brent. "Of course, you're welcome to have a look. They're probably more interesting to you than to anyone else."

"Do you know much about the building's history?" he asked. "Did your family own it before it was a bed and breakfast?"

Gran shook her head. "Goodness, no. This place sat empty for a good while before I bought it. I believe it was a rooming house way back when, but that's all I know."

Brent's eyes lit up with excitement. "A rooming house? That could explain the early entries." He turned to Felicity. "This could be an incredible resource for my research."

Gran looked at her. "Did you find the lights for the porch?"

She laughed. "In all the excitement of finding the guest books, I forgot them. I'll go get them and hang them now."

"I could help," Brent offered. "I was just taking a bit of a break when I found you sitting out on the porch of that cute outbuilding."

She smiled. "Yes, Gran insists on calling it the shed, but it's adorable, isn't it? Just like a tiny little house."

She led Brent back to the shed. His eyes sparkled with genuine interest as he spoke about the potential historical significance of the guest books. It was refreshing to see someone so passionate about their work. Had she ever been that passionate about teaching? Surely she had when she first started. If only she could find that passion again, instead of the burnout she'd felt the last few years with each day dragging on and on. Dealing with the students, the parents, the administration, and the ever-changing rules.

Pushing her thoughts away as they entered the shed, she located the box of twinkle lights and some hooks and extension cords. She picked up the boxes, and he reached for them.

"Here, let me take that." He took the boxes from her and they headed back to the B&B.

"Gran's going to be thrilled to have these up. She thinks it will make it a welcoming atmosphere out on the porch."

He chuckled. "As if it wasn't already with the rockers, and flower planters, and the great view of the bay. Your Gran really rolls out the welcome mat to her guests."

"That she does." They climbed the stairs to the porch. "I appreciate the help with these."

"I'm happy to help," he said, flashing her a warm smile that made her heart skip a beat.

What was that all about?

She quickly looked away, focusing on gathering the extension cords and hooks they'd need.

As they set to work hanging the lights along the porch railing, she found herself stealing glances at Brent. He was handsome, with a neatly trimmed haircut and kind eyes. She mentally chided herself for noticing, reminding herself that he was a guest and she was here to work, not to get distracted by a charming historian.

As they continued to string the lights, the conversation flowed easily between them. "So, how long have you worked here at the B&B?" he asked.

"Oh, I'm just here for the summer. Visiting Gran and helping out."

"So what do you do when you're not here?" He paused from untangling a strand of lights.

"I'm… a teacher."

"That's a rewarding career."

"It is… but I'm suffering a bit of burnout." She didn't know why she was telling him this. It was her burden to bear.

"It's hard when something you once loved starts to feel like a burden," he said, his tone understanding. "Sometimes a change of scenery is exactly what you need to gain a fresh perspective."

She nodded, surprised at how easily he seemed to grasp her situation. "That's what I'm hoping for. I just need to figure out what comes next."

"Well, if you ever want to talk about it, I'm a pretty good listener," he offered, his smile genuine.

She returned the smile, feeling a warmth spread through her. "I might just take you up on that."

As they finished hanging the last of the

lights, she stepped back to admire their work. The soft glow added a magical touch to the already charming porch. She glanced at Brent, who was also surveying the results with a satisfied expression.

"It looks perfect," he said, turning to face her. "Your grandmother is going to love it."

"Thanks for your help," she replied, suddenly aware of how close they were standing. She felt a flutter as their eyes met.

The spell was broken by the sound of Gran calling her from inside. She took a step back, her cheeks warming. "We should probably head in."

He nodded, a hint of a smile playing at the corners of his mouth. "After you," he said, gesturing toward the door.

She slipped past him and went inside. He headed up to his room to work, and she headed to the kitchen.

"You okay?" Gran asked.

"What? Sure. I'm fine."

"You look a little flushed."

"It's getting warm out there." And that wasn't a lie. It had been warm out there. Especially next to Brent. "But we got the lights all hung. You're right, they do look great."

"Thanks for doing that. Oh, I made some cookies. Want some?"

"Sure do." She poured herself a glass of cool water and grabbed a cookie. Gran looked at her for a long moment before turning back to washing the cookie sheet.

She never could hide anything from Gran. Not that there was really anything to hide...

CHAPTER 4

The next morning, Felicity was helping Gran serve breakfast when Brent came downstairs, holding one of the old guest books she'd found in the shed. His eyes twinkled with excitement.

"Good morning, Miss Bond, Mrs. Bond," he said, nodding to each of them. "I started looking through one of these old guest books last night. I found a really interesting entry."

Gran wiped her hands on her apron and came over to the table where he'd set the book down. "First of all, it's Felicity and Darlene. No standing on formality here. And tell us what you found."

"There's an entry here from a Prince Lawrence of Bardonzia. I looked it up, and

Bardonzia is a small territory in the Pacific Ocean. I'd never heard of it before."

Felicity leaned over to look at the entry. The handwriting was a flowing script, the ink faded with age. *Prince Lawrence of Bardonzia. September 3, 1924.* "Huh. I wonder what a prince from the Pacific was doing all the way out here on Magnolia Key back then."

Gran tapped her chin thoughtfully. "You know, I bet Dale would know something about this. He's kind of the unofficial historian around here. Knows all sorts of things about the island's history."

Brent looked up, intrigued. "Dale?"

"He runs the antique shop in town. Second Finds. He's got an entire section in the back dedicated to the history of Magnolia Key," Gran explained.

She nodded. "Yeah, if anyone would know about a visiting prince, it would be Dale. We should go talk to him."

"That's a great idea," Brent said, his eyes lighting up at the prospect of a new lead in his research.

Gran smiled. "Why don't you two head into town after breakfast? I can handle things here."

She hesitated. She'd been planning to help

Gran with some chores around the B&B. But the mystery of the prince from Bardonzia had aroused her curiosity. And spending more time with Brent wasn't an entirely unappealing idea, either.

"Are you sure, Gran? I don't want to leave you with all the work."

Gran waved her off. "Oh, don't you worry about me. I've been running this place for decades. I think I can manage for a few hours. You two go and see what you can find out about our mysterious prince."

"Thanks, Gran. We won't be gone too long."

After breakfast, she and Brent headed out to Second Finds. The bell above the door jingled as they stepped inside, announcing their arrival. Dale looked up from where he was arranging a display of vintage postcards.

"Felicity! Good to see you. I heard you were in town for the summer," he said, coming over to greet them. "And who's this?"

"Dale, this is Brent Dunn. He's a historian staying at the B&B, doing some research on the early development of southern Florida."

"Oh, you're here doing that talk in a few weeks, aren't you?" Dale shook Brent's hand.

"Pleasure to meet you. Always happy to meet a fellow history buff."

Brent smiled. "Likewise. Actually, we were hoping you might be able to help us with something."

"Oh?" Dale raised an eyebrow.

She explained about the guest book and the entry from Prince Lawrence. Dale listened intently, nodding along.

"Prince Lawrence of Bardonzia? How interesting. I've recently heard of Bardonzia. Beverly found a rolled-up painting hidden in a bookcase. When I did some research for her, I came across a photo. Give me a minute to find it."

He disappeared to the back of the shop and soon came back, waving a photo triumphantly. "Found it. Look, it's a photo of a building at their landing on Bardonzia."

She frowned. "Doesn't that look like the building that used to be here at the landing on Magnolia Key? Before it got destroyed?"

"It does look like it. And see? It has the same M and B intertwined over the doorway. I've read something about how Bardonzia was a sister island to Magnolia Key. I guess that was a thing back in the early 1900s."

"So, I guess this prince from our sister island came and stayed at the building Gran bought?"

"Sounds like it. I could do some digging around and see if I can learn more about Darlene's house. Who owned it back then. Any history about it."

"Thank you. That would be helpful."

"Let me see what I can find in my records. I've got a whole archive of old newspapers and documents in the back storage room. If There's any mention of a visiting prince, it'll be in there somewhere."

Brent's eyes lit up at the mention of the archive. "Would you mind if I took a look as well? I'd love to see what kind of historical documents you have."

"Of course, of course," Dale said, waving them toward the back of the shop. "Right this way."

As they entered the back room of Second Finds, her eyes widened at the sight of the extensive archive. Shelves lined the walls, filled with boxes of old newspapers, documents, and photographs. The musty scent of aging paper filled the air.

Dale led them to a section labeled "1920s" and began pulling out boxes. "Let's start here. If

There's any mention of Prince Lawrence, it'll likely be in the papers from the mid to late twenties."

She and Brent each took a box and began carefully sifting through the delicate pages. The rustling of paper and the occasional exclamation of discovery filled the room as they searched for any mention of the mysterious prince.

After about an hour, Brent held up a yellowed newspaper clipping. "I think I found something. Listen to this: *'Prince Lawrence of Bardonzia arrived on Magnolia Key yesterday for his biennial visit. The prince, known for his love of the island's tranquil beauty, will be staying at the Magnolia Landing Boardinghouse for the duration of his two-week stay.'"*

Felicity leaned over to look at the article. "Biennial visit? So, he came to the island every other year?"

Dale nodded, a distant look in his eyes. "You know, I think I remember reading a long time ago. Something about a scandal or misunderstanding that happened during one visit of someone famous. I wonder if it was this Prince Lawrence."

Her curiosity was piqued. "A scandal? What kind of scandal?"

Dale frowned, trying to recall the details. "I can't quite remember. It's been years since I came across that article. I'll keep looking through these boxes and see if I can find it."

They continued their search, the mystery of Prince Lawrence and the possible scandal adding a new layer of intrigue to their investigation. As they burrowed deeper into the archive, she felt a growing connection to the island's past and the secrets it held.

Hours passed as they combed through the articles, occasionally sharing interesting tidbits they found, but nothing more about the prince. Dale finally sat back, rubbing his eyes. "I'm sorry, folks. I just can't seem to find that article I remember. It's going to bother me now until I can recall the details."

Brent glanced at his watch. "It's getting late. We should probably head back to the B&B. But this has been fascinating. Thank you for letting us look through your archive, Dale."

Dale waved off the thanks. "Anytime. I love sharing this stuff with people who appreciate it. And don't worry, I'll keep digging. If I find anything more about Prince Lawrence or that scandal, I'll let you know."

She stood, stretching her back after hours of sitting hunched over the boxes. "Thanks, Dale. This has been really interesting. I had no idea Magnolia Key had such a rich history."

As they said their goodbyes and headed out of the shop, her mind was buzzing with questions. Who was Prince Lawrence? What brought him to Magnolia Key so regularly? And what was this scandal Dale had mentioned? Did it involve Prince Lawrence?

She glanced over at Brent, who seemed equally lost in thought. "Looks like you've stumbled onto quite the historical mystery," she said.

Brent smiled. "It does seem that way. I came here to research the early development of southern Florida, but this prince from Bardonzia… That's something I never expected to uncover. I'm intrigued to learn more."

She and Brent strolled back to the B&B, the late afternoon sun casting long shadows across the sidewalk. The day's discoveries had energized them both, and she found herself eager to continue their conversation.

"So, what got you interested in Florida's history?" she asked, glancing over at Brent.

"I recently found out my mother was from this area." He paused, a sad smile settling on his lips. "I didn't know her well—she died when I was just a young boy. Anyway, I lived with some of my father's relatives most of the time. Dad traveled for his work. Overseas a lot, so I didn't see him often. He's gone now too."

"I'm so sorry." Her heart broke for the little boy who lost his mom and whose father was away on business all the time.

He shrugged. "It's just how my life was. But I recently came across some old items of my mother's. That's how I found out she came from this area. That got me interested in this particular area. Anyway, I do find researching the history fascinating."

She nodded. "Even just learning about Magnolia Key's past today was eye-opening. I've been coming here my whole life but never knew about Prince Lawrence or Bardonzia."

"That's the beauty of history," Brent said. "There's always something new to uncover, even in places you think you know well."

They walked in companionable silence for a

moment, the gentle island breeze rustling through the palm trees lining the street.

"What about you?" Brent asked. "Do you come to Magnolia Key every summer?"

She hesitated, unsure how much to reveal. "I do come visit every summer, but not for the whole summer like this year. I needed to get out of the city. Get… away. Needed a break after this past school year. Thought I'd come and help Gran out at the B&B for a while."

He nodded, seeming to sense there was more to the story. "Teaching can be tough," he said gently. "I did a stint as a professor for a few years before focusing on research. It's rewarding, but it can really take it out of you."

His understanding tone made her feel unexpectedly emotional. She took a deep breath, surprised to find herself wanting to open up to him.

"It's just… I used to love it so much," she admitted. "But lately, it feels like I've lost that spark, you know? I'm not sure if I can get it back."

He listened attentively as they walked, his expression thoughtful. "Maybe spending time here on Magnolia Key is exactly what you need."

She smiled, feeling a glimmer of hope at his words. "Maybe you're right. I have to admit, today's little historical adventure was the most engaged I've felt in a long time."

They reached the B&B, pausing at the bottom of the porch steps. Brent turned to face her, his expression warm.

"Well, if you're interested, I'd love to have your help with more research while I'm here," he offered. "Your local knowledge could be invaluable, and who knows what other mysteries we might uncover?"

She felt a flutter of excitement at the prospect. "I'd like that," she said, surprised by how much she meant it.

As they climbed the porch steps together, she realized with a start that she was smiling. A real, genuine smile. And it felt good.

CHAPTER 5

The next morning, Felicity was helping Gran with the breakfast dishes when Brent entered the kitchen. "Good morning," he greeted them.

"There's some coffee if you'd like some," Gran said, waving a dishcloth at him.

"Thank you, I appreciate it." Brent poured himself a cup. "I got so engrossed in my research that I lost track of time and missed breakfast."

Felicity dried her hands on a towel and turned to face him. "I was planning to head into town for lunch at Coastal Coffee. Would you like to join me?"

His eyes lit up. "That sounds great. I'd love to."

She finished helping Gran while Brent lounged in the kitchen with his coffee. After they were done, they said goodbye to Gran and set off, walking side by side along the quiet island streets. The sun was warm on her face, and a gentle breeze carried the scent of salt and tropical flowers.

As they entered Coastal Coffee, a cheerful bell above the door announced their arrival. It had always charmed her that so many of the businesses here on the island had bells over their doors.

Beverly, the owner, looked up from behind the counter and grinned. "Felicity! So good to see you, honey." She came around to give her a big hug.

"It's great to see you too. I've been meaning to get by here to catch up with you." She returned the embrace, then gestured to Brent. "This is Brent Dunn. He's staying at the B&B while he researches the history of southern Florida."

Beverly shook Brent's hand, her eyes twinkling. "Well, welcome to Magnolia Key, Brent. You've come to the right place for history. This island is full of stories."

They settled at a table, and Beverly brought

over menus. Felicity was glad to see it was mostly the same as ever. She liked that about Coastal Coffee, about most of the island. Things didn't change much.

After they ordered, Felicity stopped Beverly as she walked past. "Can you join us for a bit?"

Beverly glanced around the cafe. "Sure, Maxine is here to help. I can take a few." She took a seat. "So I haven't seen Darlene in a while. She keeping busy with the guests?"

"She is. The B&B is mostly booked for the entire summer."

"We've been particularly full of tourists this summer. Which is good for business, but sure makes for some long hours."

"That's why I'm here to help her." She leaned forward. "And you'll never guess what we found in an old guest book at the B&B."

Beverly raised an eyebrow. "Do tell."

Brent chimed in, "There were entries from a Prince Lawrence of Bardonzia, dating back to the early 1900s. Apparently, he visited Magnolia Key regularly, and Dale mentioned some sort of scandal back then, but we don't know if it relates to Prince Lawrence or not."

Beverly's eyes widened. "Bardonzia? Dale

mentioned that country when I showed him the painting I found."

Excitement shone in Brent's eyes. "Really? We spoke to Dale at the antique shop, and he mentioned the prince too, but he didn't have many details."

Beverly nodded. "There have been a few mysterious things found around town recently. That painting I found. An old letter written in code. And a pendant that was found in a drawer in the dressing room at the theater."

Brent leaned back in his chair, his expression thoughtful. "Fascinating. I wonder if they're somehow all connected."

She felt a thrill of anticipation at the idea of digging deeper into the island's secrets. "Maybe we could ask around, see if anyone else has heard stories or found anything related to Prince Lawrence."

Beverly smiled. "You two might just uncover a century-old mystery. Magnolia Key has a way of revealing its secrets when the time is right."

As they enjoyed their lunch, they continued to discuss the intriguing mystery, and Felicity's enthusiasm grew with each new piece of information. She couldn't remember the last time she'd felt so excited about something.

"So, Beverly," Felicity said, leaning forward, "tell us more about this painting you found. What did it look like?"

Beverly took a sip of her iced tea. "It was a rolled-up canvas I discovered in an old bookcase here at the cafe. When we unrolled it, we saw a scene of a building that looked just like the one that it used to be on Magnolia Key. There was an intriguing detail —the letters M and B intertwined over the door."

Brent's eyes lit up. "M and B... Magnolia and Bardonzia, perhaps?"

She nodded, her mind full of possibilities. "That's a good theory. And you mentioned a coded letter too?"

"Yes," Beverly confirmed. "It was found in an old purse. We couldn't make sense of it at first, but I later found out it was written in some kind of family code. Ones the Whitmores used. It instructed someone to meet at the landing on a Friday night."

"Whitmore? As in Miss Eleanor?"

"Yes, it was her son, Cliff, who told me about the family code they'd used over the years." Beverly's eyes clouded briefly.

"Gran told me that Cliff is trying to get the

codes changed so he can build a high-rise building at the end of the boardwalk."

"It's not going to happen. We won't let it," Beverly said firmly. "No matter what Cliff wants."

"I hope you can stop him. That will ruin the whole feel of the island."

Beverly nodded. "Anyway, back to the mysterious items that have been showing up."

She turned to Brent. "This is incredible. We've got a mysterious prince, a coded letter, a painting of a building that looks just like one that used to be here on the island, and a pendant. They must all be connected somehow."

He nodded, his expression thoughtful. "It's like pieces of a puzzle, scattered across time. We just need to figure out how they fit together."

As they continued to talk, her excitement grew. The mystery was captivating, yes, but it was more than that. It was the thrill of discovery, the joy of learning something new. She realized how much she'd missed this feeling —the exhilaration of piecing together information, of following a trail of clues.

"You know," she said, almost to herself, "this

reminds me of why I became a teacher in the first place. I wanted to inspire curiosity, to help students uncover new knowledge."

Beverly reached across and patted her hand. "It's easy to lose sight of that initial passion sometimes. But maybe it's still there, isn't it?"

Felicity nodded, surprised by the lump in her throat. "Maybe."

Beverly rose. "Sometimes we all need a reminder of what lights us up inside. Sounds like this mystery might be just what you needed."

After Beverly left, she turned to Brent. "So, where do we start? How can we dig deeper into this mystery?"

He grinned, clearly pleased by her enthusiasm. "Well, I think our next step should be to compile all the information we have so far. Maybe we could create a timeline of events, see if we can spot any patterns or connections we might have missed."

She nodded eagerly. "That's a great idea."

"We'll use my room as our command center."

"Works for me."

As they said goodbye to Beverly and left the

cafe, she couldn't wait to get back to Gran's and get started on their research.

Late that night, Brent stood at the window in his room, gazing out at the moonlit water. The gentle lapping of the waves against the shore created a soothing rhythm that seemed to match the slower pace of life on Magnolia Key. He was growing increasingly fond of the island's peaceful atmosphere and friendly inhabitants, particularly Felicity and her grandmother, Darlene. Okay, *especially* Felicity.

He was excited to jump into researching the mysteries surrounding Prince Lawrence of Bardonzia and his connection to the island. The clues they had uncovered so far—the painting, the coded letter, and the pendant—hinted at a fascinating story waiting to be revealed. If, and that was a big if, they were all somehow connected.

But it wasn't just the thrill of the historical hunt that had Brent looking forward to the days ahead. He had to admit that he was thoroughly enjoying Felicity's company. Their conversations flowed easily, and he found himself captivated by the way her eyes sparkled with each new discovery. It was as if the island's secrets were breathing new life into her, gradually erasing the weariness he had noticed when they first met.

He smiled to himself, anticipating the time they would spend together as they continued their research. There was something about Felicity that drew him in, a kindred spirit who shared his passion for uncovering knowledge.

He couldn't wait to see where their investigation would lead them, both in terms of the island's history and their growing connection. At least *he* felt a connection to Felicity.

Did she feel anything toward him?

As he stared out the window, his mind was full of ideas for their next steps. Tomorrow, he would suggest they go to the mainland and visit the big regional library to search for any historical records that might shed light on Prince Lawrence's visits. And perhaps, if the timing was right, he would ask Felicity to join him for dinner at one of the local restaurants before heading back to the island. The thought of spending more time with her, both in and out of their research, filled him with something he hadn't felt in a long time.

He took one last look out the window, his mind still swirling with thoughts of the island's mysteries and the intriguing woman who had become his partner in unraveling them.

Brent awoke the next morning, eager to continue his research. The fact that Felicity was helping had little to do with his excitement, he was sure. He shook his head at himself. He made his way downstairs to the kitchen, where he found Felicity and her grandmother preparing breakfast for the guests.

"Good morning, Felicity, Darlene." He greeted them with a smile.

"Good morning, Brent." Felicity turned and smiled widely at him. "I was just telling Gran about our plans to investigate the Prince Lawrence mystery further."

Darlene chuckled. "You two seem to be quite the detective duo. I'm glad to see you so excited about something, Felicity."

Brent turned to Felicity. "I was thinking, maybe we could head over to the mainland today and visit the library in Sarasota. They might have some historical records that could give us more information about Prince Lawrence's visits to Magnolia Key."

Her face lit up. "That's a great idea! I'd love to go." Then she frowned. "But I promised Gran I'd help with some baking. And we were going to do a thorough cleaning of the sitting room."

Darlene waved her hand. "Don't you worry about the B&B. I've got everything under control here. You two go and enjoy your little adventure."

Felicity gave her grandmother a hug. "Thanks, Gran. You're the best."

After a quick breakfast, he and Felicity caught the ferry to the mainland. During the ride, they discussed their theories about Prince Lawrence and the potential scandal surrounding his visits. He found himself increasingly drawn to Felicity's keen intellect and her passion for uncovering the truth.

Once they arrived in Sarasota, they made their way to the library. The librarian directed them to the local history section, where they began their search. They pored over microfilm of old newspapers, city records, and historical documents, looking for any mention of Prince Lawrence or his connection to Magnolia Key.

After several hours of digging, Felicity let out a small gasp. "Brent, look at this," she whispered.

He leaned over her shoulder to scan the article. It was a society page from the 1920s detailing a grand party held at the Magnolia Landing Boardinghouse. Among the list of notable attendees was none other than Prince Lawrence of Bardonzia.

"It says here that many prominent members of the town were in attendance. I see some Whitmores on the list." She pointed to the screen.

"But nothing mentioning a scandal that Dale thought he remembered?"

"Not that I can find."

They continued their search, hoping to find more information about the prince. As they worked side by side, he found himself stealing glances at Felicity, admiring the way her brow creased in concentration and the way she bit her lip when she was deep in thought.

Hours later, he glanced at his watch and

leaned closer to her, keeping his voice low. "I'm sorry. I forget how I lose track of time when I'm working. We should probably go. We worked right through lunch."

She looked up from the old book she'd been reading on the history of the area. "Did we? I guess I lost track of time too."

They gathered their notes and prepared to leave, and he turned to her. "How about I buy you some dinner before we take the ferry back? There's a nice place on the waterfront I've been wanting to try."

"That sounds great. Now that you've reminded me we skipped lunch, I'm starving." She grinned at him.

He drove them to the wharf, and they walked along the waterfront, the warm Florida air enveloping them. The restaurant, a charming seafood spot called The Salty Pelican, sat perched on stilts overlooking the bay. Its weathered wood exterior and string lights gave it a cozy, inviting atmosphere.

As they approached the hostess stand, he noticed how the sun cast a golden glow on Felicity's hair. He cleared his throat, pushing away the distracting thought.

"Table for two, please," he said to the hostess.

They were led to a table on the covered outdoor deck, offering a stunning view of the water. Brent pulled out Felicity's chair for her, earning a warm smile of thanks.

"This is lovely," she said, taking in the view. "I can't believe I've never been here before."

Brent settled into his own seat and picked up the menu. "I'm glad you like it. I've heard great things about their seafood."

They perused the menu, and when the waiter arrived, both opted for the fried grouper with a side of hush puppies. As they waited for their food, Brent found himself captivated by the delight in Felicity's eyes as she looked out at the view.

"This really is beautiful," she said, turning back to him. "Thank you for bringing me here."

He nodded, feeling a warmth spread through his chest. "I'm glad you're enjoying it. It's nice to share this with someone who appreciates it as much as I do."

A gentle breeze carried the salty scent of the ocean, ruffling her hair. She tucked a strand behind her ear, her fingers lingering for a moment on the sea glass necklace she wore. It was a small detail, but it struck him as quintessentially Floridian.

The clink of glasses and murmur of conversations around them created a cozy atmosphere. He found himself relaxing in her company. He watched as she absently traced patterns on the condensation of her water glass, seemingly lost in thought.

"Penny for your thoughts?" he asked, breaking the comfortable silence between them.

She looked up, a small smile playing on her lips. "Oh, I was just thinking about how nice this is. It's been a while since I've had a dinner out like this."

"Me, too. This is nice."

"So," she began, "you mentioned earlier that your mother had roots in this area and that's why you're so interested in the local history."

He nodded, leaning back in his chair. "Partly, yes. To be honest, I don't know much about my mother. I guess…" He shrugged. "It's my way to try to feel closer to her? I've always been curious about her life and her family history."

Their food arrived, interrupting their conversation. A mouthwatering aroma filled the air as the server set down steaming plates of golden-fried grouper and hush puppies. They both took a moment to enjoy the first bites before Brent continued.

"My father didn't talk about her much. I think it was too painful for him. But I do know she grew up somewhere along this part of the coast."

She nodded, listening intently. "Do you know anything else about her?"

He took a sip of his iced tea. "Not much. Right before I left to come here, I found an old photo of her standing on a beach. There's a lighthouse in the background, but I haven't had time to identify which one it is. And I don't know if that's where she lived, or just somewhere she was visiting."

"That's fascinating," she said. "Maybe we could try and find out which lighthouse it is while you're here. There are quite a few along this stretch of coast."

"I'd like that. Thank you." He paused, then convinced himself to continue. "I've really enjoyed working with you. Doing all this research. It's so much more… enjoyable… with someone else." Especially when that someone was Felicity.

She smiled back at him. "It has been fun, hasn't it? And it's so exciting when we find more little clues, like that party at Magnolia Landing Boardinghouse. I wonder why Prince Lawrence stayed at a boardinghouse instead of an inn?"

"I don't know. Maybe there wasn't an inn back then?" he suggested.

"Maybe. We could look into that too."

"Sounds like we have hours and hours of research ahead of us."

"It does, doesn't it?" She smiled at him and didn't seem bothered by that prospect.

They enjoyed a leisurely meal, then left to take the ferry back to Magnolia Key. The excitement of their research trip still buzzed between them. As he drove onto the ferry and put his car in park, he turned to her. "Want to go up to the top deck?" he asked. "We might catch a nice sunset."

Felicity's eyes lit up. "That sounds perfect."

They made their way up the stairs to the open-air deck. A warm breeze buffeted them as they found a spot along the railing. The sky was ablaze with oranges and pinks, the sun a glowing orb sinking toward the horizon.

"It's beautiful," she breathed, leaning against the railing.

Brent nodded in agreement, but found his gaze drawn more to her than the sunset. The fading light cast a glow on her face, highlighting the contentment in her expression.

"Thank you for today," she said, turning to look at him. "I haven't felt this… alive in a long time."

"I'm glad," he replied, pleased that he'd been able to do this for her. "I've enjoyed every minute of it."

They fell into a comfortable silence as the sun dipped lower, painting the water with streaks of glistening gold. His hand rested on the railing, mere inches from hers. He was acutely aware of the small distance between them.

As the ferry cut through a wave, the deck shifted slightly. Her hand slid along the railing, brushing against his. A jolt of electricity seemed to pass between them at the contact. Neither pulled away.

His heart did a double beat as he made a decision. Slowly, carefully, he turned his hand, gently taking hers in his own. Her skin was soft and warm against his palm. He held his breath, waiting for her reaction.

Her fingers curled around his, returning the

gentle pressure. He exhaled softly, a smile tugging at his lips. He glanced at her, only to find her looking up at him with a shy smile of her own.

They stood there, hand in hand, watching as the last sliver of sun disappeared beneath the horizon. The sky darkened, and stars began to twinkle overhead. Neither spoke, but he felt as though something significant had shifted between them.

CHAPTER 7

"You look chipper this morning," Gran greeted her when she entered the kitchen and grabbed an apron. "Sleep well?"

"Very well." She busied herself helping Gran, humming under her breath as she pulled a batch of sticky buns from the oven. Her mind kept going back to last night. Brent's simple move of taking her hand. That was all, just a simple connection between them. She paused and stared out the window, remembering how lovely spending the day with Brent had been.

Gran looked at her and grinned. "Humming now, are we? You sure don't seem like the same woman who came here just a short while ago."

"I don't feel like the same woman," she admitted. "I was exhausted and disillusioned and… well, it felt like everything in my life was going wrong."

"And now?"

"Now, I feel like…" The warmth of a blush crept across her cheeks. "I feel like things are turning around."

"So you haven't said much about it, but I guess it was a really tough school year? You feel like talking about it?"

"It was. You know, when I was little, we had tornado drills where we were taught to go under our desks for protection or fire drills where we all filed outside? Now we have safety drills for… active shooters. Lock the doors and stay away from windows. It doesn't seem like kids should have to grow up with those kinds of drills."

Gran walked over and touched her arm. "No, it isn't right that they have to deal with all that at such a young age."

"And I had a handful of parents this year that were, how do I put this nicely? Very vocal. About… everything." She shrugged, thinking back on Mrs. Dixon in particular. She could not do anything right in Mrs. Dixon's eyes. And her son, Jeff, was a handful, but Mrs. Dixon insisted he never did anything wrong. Not even when he'd punched poor Jenny and given her a black eye. Even the principal seemed afraid to stand up to Mrs. Dixon.

Then there was the time Mrs. Dixon went to the school board, threatening to get her fired. And the sad thing? She hadn't been sure if that would have been a bad thing or not.

"I'm sorry you had such a tough year. You used to come here on your summer break, all excited, telling me stories about your kids. Your eyes lit up, and you were just so happy."

"I was. But that seems like such a long time ago. The administrative part of teaching seems overwhelming now. I just… I just want to teach the kids. Get them excited about learning."

"Maybe it's time to move on. Do something different," Gran suggested gently.

"But what would I do? I've been a teacher ever since I left college. I feel like it's part of what I am. Who I am."

"Maybe this summer will give you time to sort all that out."

"I hope so because I don't think I can go through another school year like last year." She shook her head. "Enough about that. Let me bring a plate of these sticky buns out to the guests. They smell delicious." And with that, she pushed all thoughts of the school year far from her mind.

Darlene was kind of sorry she'd brought up Felicity's school year. Though it would be good if her granddaughter would actually talk about it a bit. It might make her sort it out. Come to a decision. Felicity had her whole future ahead of her—she didn't need to work at a job that made her miserable.

When Felicity left the kitchen after cleaning up the breakfast dishes, there was a noticeable spring in her step. It warmed her heart to see her granddaughter's smile, a genuine one that had been absent for far too long. The sparkle in her eyes when she talked about Brent and their research an unmistakable glimmer of the old Felicity, the one who had been so passionate about teaching and learning.

She worried about her granddaughter, though. Felicity had always been a dedicated teacher, pouring her heart and soul into her work. But over the years, Darlene had witnessed the light in Felicity's eyes dimming, the weight of burnout slowly crushing her spirit. It pained her to see Felicity so lost and disconnected from the joy she once found in her profession.

But then Brent arrived at the B&B, and she was noticing a change in Felicity. The way she lit up when discussing their research, the excitement in her voice as she recounted their discoveries—it was like watching a flower bloom after a long, harsh winter. Brent seemed to have awakened something in Felicity, a purpose and curiosity that had been dormant for far too long.

She smiled to herself as she finished tidying up the kitchen. Brent was a fine man, indeed. Polite, intelligent, and genuinely interested in the island's history. But more than that, he seemed to understand Felicity in a way that others didn't. He listened to her, valued her input, and encouraged her to explore her interests. It was a partnership that brought out the best in both of them.

As she wiped down the counters, she felt a burgeoning hope for Felicity's future. Maybe this summer on Magnolia Key would be the turning point her granddaughter needed. A chance to rediscover her passions and to find a new direction in life. And if Brent played a role in that journey, well, she certainly wouldn't object.

She glanced out the window, catching a glimpse of Felicity and Brent walking together, deep in conversation. The sight brought a smile to her face. Yes, Magnolia Key had a way of revealing what people were searching for, even if they didn't know it themselves. And for Felicity, it seemed that the island was working its magic once again.

CHAPTER 8

Brent sat working on some research as he ate his breakfast. Felicity caught a few moments here and there to chat with him as she waited on the guests, but mostly they were really busy. After things slowed down, she grabbed a cup of coffee and sat down with him.

"Sorry I couldn't help with the research this morning. It was like every guest decided to come have their breakfast at the same time."

Brent laughed. "It was rather busy, wasn't it? I think I'm going to go and talk to Dale this morning. See if he's found out anything. Then, maybe I'll catch lunch at Coastal Coffee. Want to join me?"

She nodded. "That would be great. I'd love to see what else Dale has found." She glanced at the clock on the wall. "We're about wrapped up here."

They walked the short distance to Second Finds. Dale looked up from where he was sorting through a box of old books. "Ah, Felicity and Brent. I was hoping you'd stop by today."

"Morning, Dale," she said. "We were hoping you might have some new information for us about the boardinghouse?"

Dale nodded, setting aside the books and gesturing for them to follow him to the back of the store. "I did some digging through the old records and found out that back in the early 1920s, the Magnolia Landing Boardinghouse also served as an inn for a while."

Brent looked thoughtful. "Really? I hadn't come across that in any of my research."

"Apparently, the main inn on the island was damaged pretty badly in a hurricane around that time. While it was being rebuilt, most of the visitors to Magnolia Key stayed at the boardinghouse instead."

"Really? That's kind of cool that the house has always been used as some sort of inn or B&B through the years. Thanks for finding that out for us."

Dale shrugged, a smile tugging at the corner

of his mouth. "It's what I do. Always happy to help uncover a bit more of the island's history. Oh, and here." He handed Brent a folder. "I found some articles on the island during that time period. Never know what else you might find out. Just return the folder when you're finished with it."

"This is great, thank you."

She felt a thrill of excitement run through her. Every new piece of information they uncovered only made the mystery surrounding the prince's connection to the island more intriguing. She glanced at her watch, realizing how much time had passed.

She and Brent thanked Dale for his help, and he smiled. "Make sure you let me know if you find out anything else."

"We will," Brent assured him.

They left Second Finds and headed for Coastal Coffee. As they entered, Beverly looked up from behind the counter and grinned. "Well, look who it is. How are you two doing today?"

"We're good," Felicity said, returning her smile. "Just stopping in for some lunch."

"Take a seat anywhere you like. I'll be right over."

Felicity led Brent to a table near the window,

and as they sat down, she noticed Miss Eleanor eating at a nearby table. The older woman glanced up, her sharp gaze assessing them before she returned to her meal. Felicity sat up straighter in her chair and straightened a flyaway lock of hair.

Brent leaned in and asked, "Everything okay? You have a look on your face. Like you just got caught misbehaving or something."

She laughed softly. "That's Miss Eleanor." She nodded toward the woman's table. "She used to scare me as a child. Always seemed to be judging me, like I wasn't doing what I should be doing. I felt like I always was lacking. And, to be honest, maybe she still scares me a bit."

Brent chuckled. "Sounds like a formidable woman."

"You have no idea. No one ever says no to Miss Eleanor's requests, that's for sure."

Beverly approached their table. "What can I get for you two today?"

They placed their orders, and as Beverly walked away, Felicity glanced at Miss Eleanor again. The older woman was watching them, a curious expression on her face. She quickly looked away, focusing on Brent instead.

"So, what do you think about the

information Dale gave us?" she asked, trying to ignore the feeling of Miss Eleanor's gaze.

Brent leaned forward. "It's fascinating. I had no idea the boardinghouse had served as an inn during that time period. I can't wait to look over the file Dale gave me."

They continued to discuss the possibilities, their voices low and heads bent together. Felicity found herself drawn in by Brent's enthusiasm and the way his mind worked, always seeking out new angles and connections.

As they talked, she felt a growing connection to Brent. It was more than just their shared interest in the island's history. There was something about him that made her feel seen and understood.

Beverly returned with their food, and they dug in, savoring the delicious flavors. A warmth spread through her, a combination of the good food, the company, and the sense of purpose that came with their investigation.

As they finished, she saw that Miss Eleanor was still sitting at her table, sipping on coffee. "You know, we could go ask Miss Eleanor about what we've found out. Tell her about Prince Lawrence. She might know something. Her family has been on the island for generations. And it did say some Whitmores were at that party along with Prince Lawrence." She laughed. "Though, I admit, I'm a little scared to go over there and ask her."

He grinned. "Come on. We can do this." They got up and crossed over to Miss Eleanor's table.

"Good afternoon, Miss Eleanor."

"Hello, Felicity. Darlene said you were coming to the island to help her this summer. Surprised to see you out on a date instead."

There, that was it. The sense of judgment. "No, it's not a date—" She blushed. "This is Brent Dunn. He's here doing some research on the history of the area."

"Ah, yes. The fellow giving the talk soon."

Brent held out his hand. "That's me."

Miss Eleanor reached her hand out and shook his. "Glad to meet you. It's important we learn more about our heritage and try to preserve it."

"Yes, ma'am. And… we were wondering. We found out that Darlene's B&B used to be a boardinghouse back in the early 1920s. We found some old guest books and there was a Prince Lawrence that visited regularly. I know it's before your time, but did you ever hear anything about him?"

Miss Eleanor looked startled for a moment before she quickly covered it up. "Lawrence?" She shook her head. "No, I don't think so. A prince, you say?"

"Yes, from Bardonzia. A small island in the Pacific."

"I see." Miss Eleanor stood. "I'm sorry to cut this short, but I need to go. Have an appointment."

"Okay, well, thank you," she said. Why was she thanking the woman? She'd insinuated Felicity was shirking her responsibilities and then didn't even have any information to give them.

Miss Eleanor left, and she turned to Brent. "Did you get the feeling she was surprised when you brought up Prince Lawrence's name?"

He frowned. "I did. Like she knew of him but didn't want to talk about it."

"Told you she was scary." She laughed. "Come on. I should get back to the B&B and help Gran."

They paid their bill and headed outside. She glanced up at the sky. "Looks like we might be getting a storm coming in."

"It does. We should hurry or we're going to get caught out in it."

"I'd almost forgotten how quickly storms pop up here on the island. Swoop in, dump buckets of rain, then just as quickly head out and the sun comes back out."

He took her hand as they walked briskly back to the B&B. They raced up the driveway just as the first raindrops were starting to fall.

CHAPTER 9

As Felicity and Brent entered the B&B, Gran greeted them. "Glad you two made it back before the storm hit." She glanced out the window at the darkening sky. "Looks like it's going to be a doozy."

She nodded, relieved they'd beaten the rain. "We were just at Coastal Coffee when we noticed the clouds rolling in."

"Good thing you didn't linger too long, then." The lights flickered and Gran frowned. "I was about to go searching for the battery-powered lanterns. Would you mind helping me? They should be in the storage room. I want to have them handy, just in case."

"Of course." Brent nodded. "Glad to help."

As Felicity led the way to the storage room,

the lights flickered ominously. Gran's voice called out, "Better hurry and find those lanterns. We might need them sooner than we thought."

She began rummaging through the shelves, past canned peaches and Gran's strawberry jam in neat rows of glass jars, and boxes of paper products. She scanned the shelves, looking for the familiar shape of the lanterns. Brent looked at a set of shelves just to her left. Just as she thought she'd found them, the lights went out completely, plunging them into darkness.

A startled gasp escaped her lips. A wave of unease washed over her as the darkness pressed in from all sides. But then Brent's warm voice broke through the silence. "It's okay. I'm right over here. Say something and I'll come to you."

"I'm over here."

Soon she felt the gentle pressure of his hand on her arm, steadying her. The simple gesture sent a flutter through her, and she was grateful for the darkness that hid the blush creeping up her cheeks.

Brent took out his phone, the soft glow of the screen illuminating their surroundings. In the faint light, she spotted the lanterns on a nearby shelf. She reached out and grabbed them, handing some to Brent.

His fingers brushed against hers as he took the lantern. Again, she was grateful for the dim light as the warmth of another blush flooded her cheeks. She reached out and grabbed some more lanterns.

She needed to get a grip on this blushing thing.

Brent turned on one of the lanterns and held it high. They made their way back to the kitchen, the lantern casting a gentle glow in the darkened inn. Gran looked up as they entered, relief evident on her face. "Ah, good."

Brent set the lantern on the counter, its light pushing back the shadows. "We found them, Darlene. Looks like you're prepared for whatever this storm brings."

"I need to go knock on everyone's door and offer them a lantern. And I'll put some by the front door to give anyone when they come back if they aren't here."

"I'll bring the lanterns to the guests," Felicity offered, not wanting Gran walking around in the dim light.

"I'll help you," Brent insisted.

They each grabbed a few lanterns and headed upstairs, the light from the lanterns casting dancing shadows on the walls.

"I'll take the east wing if you want to cover the west," Brent suggested.

She nodded, grateful for his efficiency. "Sounds good. Meet you back here when we're done?"

As she made her way down the hallway, she knocked on each door, offering a lantern to the guests inside. Most were grateful for the extra light, though a few showed her that they had come prepared with their own flashlights.

She'd never been that organized when she traveled, she thought wryly. Just last year when she came to the island, she'd forgotten her swimsuit of all things. Gran had just laughed and sent her off to go shop for a new one.

When she reached the last room in her section, there was no answer to her knock. She tried again, calling out softly, "Hello? It's Felicity from the front desk. I have a lantern for you if you need one."

Still no response. She carefully placed the lantern on the floor next to the door, hoping the guests would find it when they returned.

She met Brent back at the top of the stairs. "Any luck with yours?"

He shook his head. "One room didn't

answer. I left a lantern outside their door too. Ready to head back down?"

They descended the stairs by lanternlight. Gran was waiting for them in the kitchen.

"How did it go?" she asked.

"We got most of the rooms," she replied. "Two didn't answer, so we left lanterns outside their doors."

Gran nodded. "Good thinking. I'm going to sit in the front room in case any other guests come back, though I hope they all just take shelter somewhere and let it blow over. Why don't you two do what you want for a while? There's not much else to do until the power comes back on."

She glanced at Brent, unsure of what to suggest. Gran's eyes twinkled as she added, "You know, you could take a couple glasses of wine and go up to the lookout room. It's a great place to watch the storm roll in."

She turned to Brent. "What do you think? Want to storm-watch for a bit? I used to love going up there and watching the storms when I was younger."

"Sounds perfect."

Gran shooed them toward the wine rack.

"Go on, then. I've got things covered down here."

Felicity selected a bottle of red wine, and Brent nodded in agreement. She grabbed two glasses and an opener while Brent picked up a lantern. With the small circle of light to show the way, they carefully climbed the stairs. At the top, she opened the door, revealing a cozy space with windows on all sides.

As they entered, a flash of lightning illuminated the room, followed by a low rumble of thunder. She set the wine and glasses on a small table near the window and Brent placed the lantern nearby.

"Wow," Brent breathed, taking in the panoramic view of the stormy sky and churning waves. "This is incredible."

She smiled at his look of awe. "It really is something, isn't it?"

She poured them each a glass of wine and flicked off the lantern, giving their eyes a moment to adjust to the dim light. She led him over to the window seat and they settled on it, watching as the storm intensified outside. The wind howled around the corners of the house, and rain lashed against the windows.

"I've always loved watching storms," she

said, her voice soft against the backdrop of the raging storm. "There's something so powerful and mesmerizing about them."

He nodded, his gaze fixed on the swirling clouds outside. "I know what you mean. It's like watching nature's raw energy putting on a display."

A flash of lightning illuminated the room, casting sharp shadows across their faces. Felicity counted silently in her head, waiting for the inevitable crash of thunder. When it came, even though she was expecting it, the loud crash made her jump, her wine sloshing dangerously close to the rim of her glass.

He moved closer and wrapped an arm around her shoulders, steadying her. "It's okay," he murmured, his breath warm against her ear.

She leaned into him, relishing the solid strength of his body against hers. Another flash of lightning lit up the sky, and she glanced up at him, her heart skipping a beat at the intensity in his eyes as he stared down at her.

For a brief, breathless moment, she thought he might kiss her. And in that instant, she realized that she wanted him to. The thought sent a thrill through her, a warmth that had nothing to do with the wine spreading through her veins.

But instead, he simply pulled her closer, his arm tightening around her as they sat there, watching the storm in contented silence. The wind continued to howl, the rain a constant patter against the windows, but inside, in the warmth of Brent's embrace, she felt safe and protected.

They stayed like that, watching the storm until the lightning became more distant and the thunder faded to a low rumble. Finally, he spoke, his voice a soft murmur in the quiet of the room. "Thank you for sharing this with me. I can't remember the last time I just stopped and watched a storm. It was nice." He smiled at her. "And I enjoyed the company too."

She smiled, tilting her head to look up at him. "It was nice, wasn't it?"

He returned her smile, reaching up to brush a stray lock of hair from her face. The gesture was tender, intimate, and her heart filled with an emotion she wasn't quite ready to name.

As the last of the storm faded away, they remained there, wrapped in each other's arms, the silence between them brimming with potential.

CHAPTER 10

Felicity woke to the sound of voices downstairs. She glanced at the clock, realizing she'd slept later than usual. The events of last night—the storm, the wine, and sitting in the window seat with Brent—flooded back, and a smile crept across her face.

She dressed quickly and headed down to the kitchen, where Gran was bustling about, preparing breakfast.

"Good morning, sleepyhead," Gran teased. "I was beginning to wonder if you'd join us at all."

"Us?" she asked, pouring herself a cup of coffee.

"The knitting club, remember? They'll be here any minute."

She'd completely forgotten the knitting club was coming today. "Oh, right. Do you need help setting up?"

Gran shook her head. "Everything's ready. Why don't you join us today? It's been ages since you picked up those needles."

She hesitated. It had been years since she'd knitted anything. But the idea of sitting with a group of women, creating something with her hands, suddenly appealed to her. "You know what? I think I will."

Gran beamed. "Wonderful! Pick out some yarn from my stash in the closet, and I'll grab you some needles when I see what you pick out."

As she rummaged through Gran's impressive collection of yarn, the chatter of arriving women filled the air. She selected a soft, variegated blue yarn that reminded her of the ocean and joined the group in the sunroom.

Familiar faces, along with some newcomers, greeted her warmly as she walked in with her yarn. Mrs. Thompson was still in the group and gave her big hug. "My first grandchild was just born. I'm busy knitting sweaters and booties for her."

"Congratulations." She hugged her back. "You must be thrilled."

"Oh, I am. Nothing better than being a grandmother."

Sally Ann was knitting a pair of socks and held them up. "Always a new pair of socks."

Gran introduced a woman she didn't recognize. "Felicity, this is Amanda. She's new to the island and we convinced her to join us. She helped organize the Heritage Festival a while back. Amanda, this is my granddaughter, Felicity."

Amanda smiled. "Nice to meet you. They did convince me to join them, but I'm afraid I'm still really a beginner."

"Oh, good. Then I'll have some company in the beginner section." She grinned as she showed the yarn she'd picked out to Gran.

Gran dug around in her knitting bag and handed her a pair of wooden needles. "Here you go, dear. Why don't you start with something simple? A scarf, perhaps?" She dug into her bag again and pulled out a worn sheet of paper. "That yarn will work perfectly with this pattern. It's a small triangular scarf."

She nodded and glanced at the instructions

as she took the pattern. She could do this. Maybe.

Her fingers fumbled slightly as she cast on stitches. It had been so long, but muscle memory slowly kicked in. As she began to knit, the rhythmic motion soothed her, and she found herself relaxing into the familiar routine. The smooth yarn slipped between her fingers as she tried to tension it like Gran had taught her.

The women around her chatted easily about local gossip, upcoming events, and their current knitting projects. She listened, occasionally contributing to the conversation, but mostly enjoying the feeling of community that filled the room.

"How are you enjoying your time back on Magnolia Key, Felicity?" Mrs. Thompson asked, breaking into her concentration on her stitches.

"It's been wonderful. I'd forgotten how much I love it here."

"And we hear you've been spending time with that handsome historian staying here at the B&B," another woman chimed in, her eyes twinkling.

Her cheeks grew warm. "We've been researching some local history together," she said, trying to keep her voice neutral.

"I see." The woman exchanged knowing glances with the others.

"What kind of research?" Amanda asked as she looked up from her work.

She paused her knitting, careful not to drop a stitch as she looked up at Amanda. "We've been researching a prince who stayed right here in Gran's house during the 1920s," she explained. "Prince Lawrence of Bardonzia. He visited the island several times during that decade."

Amanda leaned forward, obviously intrigued. "A prince? Here on Magnolia Key? That must have caused quite a stir."

She nodded, her fingers absently tracing the stitches on her scarf. "I'm sure it did. We found an old guest book with his name in it, and there are a few other clues scattered around town. It's been fascinating piecing it all together."

"Have you learned much about why he came here?" Mrs. Thompson asked, her knitting needles clicking steadily.

She was jealous that Mrs. Thompson could actually knit and talk at the same time. "Not as much as we'd like. We know he attended a grand party at this very house when it was the

Magnolia Landing Boardinghouse. But the details are still a bit fuzzy."

She hesitated for a moment, then continued. "We actually asked Miss Eleanor about Prince Lawrence, thinking she might know something given her family's long history on the island. But she said she knew nothing about it."

She frowned slightly, remembering Miss Eleanor's odd reaction. "To be honest, I got the feeling she was hiding something. She became quite evasive and left rather abruptly when we brought up the prince's name."

A few of the women exchanged glances, and Gran gave her a pointed look. "Eleanor likes to keep things to herself, and we should respect her privacy."

Felicity felt a flicker of guilt. She hadn't meant to gossip about Miss Eleanor. "You're right, Gran. I shouldn't have said anything."

"It's all right, dear. I know you're just excited about your research. Eleanor must have her reasons for keeping whatever she knows to herself, and it's not our place to pry." It still surprised her to hear Gran call Miss Eleanor just *Eleanor*. She was fairly certain Gran was the only person in town who called her that.

The other women nodded in agreement, and she noticed a few of them seemed to relax a bit. She wondered if they knew more about Miss Eleanor's past than they were letting on.

"Well, prince or no prince, it sounds like you're having quite the adventure," Amanda said, skillfully steering the conversation back to safer ground. "I'd love to hear more about what you've discovered so far."

Grateful for the change of subject, she launched into a detailed account of their findings and the items that other residents had found recently, from the mysterious painting to the coded letter. She told them about Gran's house being used as a boardinghouse when the inn on the island was damaged in a storm. As she spoke, she realized how much she was enjoying this historical treasure hunt.

The knitting group listened attentively, asking questions and offering suggestions. She appreciated the collective wisdom of these women, many of whom had lived on Magnolia Key for decades.

As the morning wore on, her fingers grew more confident with the knitting needles, and she fell into an easy rhythm of knitting and conversation. She glanced up and saw Gran smiling at her, and she smiled back. Yes, coming to the island for the summer had been a smart decision.

CHAPTER 11

Brent headed downstairs to find Felicity. He had to admit that he was a bit apprehensive. The other night during the storm, he'd felt very connected to her. But yesterday, she'd been so busy with the knitting club and helping Darlene that they didn't have a chance to talk at all. He'd gone over to the nearby town of Moonbeam Bay, did some research, and went to the historical alcove at the re-opened Cabot Hotel. It had been late when he made it back to Magnolia Key and he hadn't wanted to disturb Felicity at that hour.

But today he wanted to see her. Talk to her. See if the connection was still there, or was it something he'd imagined.

He approached Felicity as she cleared a

table after breakfast. "Morning." He was pleased she greeted him with a warm smile.

"Good morning, Brent. There's still some breakfast in the kitchen. I could get you some."

"No, don't go to any trouble. But I really should watch the time when I'm doing research. Looks like I missed the actual breakfast time again. I'll grab an early lunch."

"You sure?"

"I'm sure. And I was thinking about heading over to Dale's shop to look through more of his historical files. Would you like to join me?" *Say yes.*

She looked up, her eyes apologetic. "I'd love to, but Gran asked me to watch the B&B while she runs some errands. I promised her I would."

He nodded, disappointed. "No worries. I can handle the research on my own for a bit. You take care of things here."

"I miss working with you. Guess we just both got busy. But be sure to let me know if you find out anything interesting."

"Will do. Maybe we can connect back up later."

"I'd like that."

With that, he turned and went outside, stepping onto the porch. A few couples sat out on the comfortable chairs on the deck, enjoying their coffee. A fishing boat chugged by out on the bay. Just simple things that made him smile. Of course, a lot of things made him smile since he'd come to the island.

The short walk to Second Finds allowed him to enjoy the nice breeze and the quaint charm of Magnolia Key's main street. He entered the shop, the bell above the door announcing his arrival.

Dale looked up from behind the counter, a smile spreading across his face. "Brent! Good to see you again. How's the research going?"

He approached the counter, returning Dale's smile. "It's going well, thanks to your help. I was hoping to take another look through your historical files, if that's all right."

"Of course! You know you're always welcome to dig through them. Find anything particularly interesting so far?" Dale asked.

"Not a lot. And I went over to Moonbeam Bay yesterday to do some research on that area. Can't have the whole book I'm working on just be about Magnolia Key." He grinned. "Anyway, I'm back today to try and see if I can find out more about Lawrence's visits."

"Feel free to dig through any of the boxes in

the back. Most are labeled, but I do have some that are just piled there because I haven't had time to go through them and sort and file."

"Thanks, Dale."

"Anytime. It's not every day we get a historian digging into the island's past. If There's anything else I can do to help, just let me know."

With a grateful nod, he made his way to the back of the shop, where Dale kept his collection of historical documents and records. He settled in, ready to immerse himself in the search for more clues about Prince Lawrence and his connection to Magnolia Key.

Darlene walked up the winding path to Eleanor's house, admiring the meticulously tended garden. Eleanor could not abide by an errant weed or withered blossom, and her garden shone under her caring hand. She swore the flowers seemed to stand at attention, each petal perfectly aligned as if waiting for Eleanor to come out and inspect them.

She knocked on the door, and Winston's excited barking came from inside. Eleanor opened the door, her silver hair neatly pinned back. "Darlene, come on in. I'm glad you called. I've just put the kettle on for tea."

As she stepped inside, Winston bounded over, his whole body wiggling in excitement and tail swishing through the air. She bent down to pet him, her knees protesting slightly, and scratched behind his ears. "Hello, Winston. You're looking as handsome as ever."

Eleanor led her to the sitting room, where a tray with a teapot and cups awaited them. As she poured the tea, Eleanor glanced at Darlene. "I was expecting that you'd call."

"You were?"

"Of course. Ever since I gave Felicity a non-answer to her question about Prince Lawrence. I could tell she knew I wasn't telling the whole truth. I knew you'd come to call."

She nodded, accepting the cup of tea. "Yes, that is why I came to visit. I feel terrible that I know something that could help solve their mystery. But it's not my story to tell." She sighed, taking a sip of the warm, fragrant liquid. "I'm afraid they are close to finding out on their own, though."

Eleanor settled into her chair, her expression pensive. "I suppose it was only a matter of time.

The past has a way of resurfacing, no matter how deeply we try to bury it." She tapped her fingers on the armrest, a habit Darlene had seen countless times over the years.

"Felicity and Brent are determined to uncover the truth about Prince Lawrence's connection to Magnolia Key," she said, setting her cup down on the saucer. "At first, I was pleased that Felicity was helping Brent. It seemed to pull her out of her... mood. I've never seen her like how she was when she first got to the island this summer. Just not herself. Worn out. But since working with Brent, her eyes light up again. But they've already found so many clues. I worry that they'll stumble upon the whole story soon."

Eleanor's gaze drifted to the window, where the sunlight filtered through the lace curtains. "It's a delicate situation, Darlene."

She leaned forward, her voice soft. "I understand your reservations. But maybe it's time for the truth to come out? Come out on your timetable instead of from someone else?"

"I had hoped to take the secret to my grave. I can't abide by scandal tied to the Whitmore name." Eleanor's eyes met hers, a flicker of uncertainty in their depths. "And you know

Jenna? The woman who recently moved to town?"

"Of course."

"She and Nash found some letters hidden in the floorboards of her cottage when she was renovating it."

"She did? I haven't heard a word about it."

"The letters were… Vera's."

"Vera?" Her eyes widened in surprise. "Your great-aunt's?"

"Yes, Vera lived in that cottage for a while. I guess when she was… ah… communicating with Lawrence." Eleanor let out a small sigh. "Jenna did say they would keep it secret, though. Not tell anyone."

"That was good of them. But still, more and more information is showing up." She looked directly at Eleanor. "And I feel horrible keeping what I know from Felicity and Brent when they're researching so hard to find out the whole connection to the island and its history."

"Who knew the secret I told you so long ago when we were just schoolgirls would come to light so many years later?" Eleanor frowned. "I do feel badly putting you in the middle of all this. But I need some time to think about how to approach this. It's not a decision I can make lightly."

She reached out, placing a hand on Eleanor's arm. "Of course. Take all the time you need. Just know that I'm here for you, no matter what you decide."

As they finished their tea, the conversation turned to lighter topics—the upcoming events on the island, the latest gossip from the knitting club, and the big storm that came through the other day. But the unspoken truth lingered in the room, a reminder that the past had a way of shaping the present, no matter how hard they tried to keep it hidden.

Long after Darlene left, Eleanor sat in her parlor with Winston at her feet. She strongly disliked that Darlene was caught in the middle of all this. Had she known all those years ago when she had confided in Darlene that it would all come up at this stage of their lives, she would have kept the secret to herself. Her own family had rarely talked about it. After Vera left, it was like she never existed.

She didn't know what really happened. If

Vera had left on her own, or if they'd sent her away to avoid any scandal. She had overheard her father talking about Vera a few times. Mentioning what a disappointment Vera was and if the town found out, their name would be disgraced.

And after Jenna had come to her with the letters she found hidden in her cottage, Eleanor knew that the scraps of conversations she'd heard over the years were true. Vera and Lawrence were involved. How involved, she wasn't certain.

She'd never found out where Vera went or what happened to her. She might never find out. All she knew was her family was bound and determined to keep whatever Vera did and whatever happened to her a secret.

And so far, they'd managed to do that over the years. But that Brent fellow was a sharp one. He knew how to do his research. He was bound to find out about the pendant. The one Tori had found in the theater. Vera's pendant.

There had been some scandal about how the pendant had gone missing. Accusations thrown around.

Only, the pendant hadn't been stolen or lost. Lawrence had secretly given it to Vera. As the years went by, Vera actually wore it in a production at the theater. Not that anyone knew she was wearing *that* pendant. To her, it sounded like a gutsy move, but then she'd heard her father say that Vera didn't have a lick of sense.

But if all this came out, the Whitmore name would be tarnished. She didn't want that. But she also didn't want Darlene to have to keep secrets from her granddaughter or feel like she was lying to Felicity.

The lie of omission. She knew about that one herself.

She let out a long sigh. Why couldn't things like this just be kept in the past? Buried where they belonged.

Winston rolled over and stared up at her as if he was empathizing with her, his tail thumping slowly against the floor. She reached down and petted him and he settled back down for another snooze. He was getting older and slowing down some—but then, so was she.

CHAPTER 12

Felicity was cleaning the front room when Brent came back from Dale's late that afternoon.

A wide smile spread across his face when he saw her. "Oh, good. There you are. I had a great research day. Found out some more things about Lawrence. Want to grab a quick drink and I'll tell you what I found?"

"I'd love to. Let me just finish tidying up this room."

"Perfect. I have a bottle of wine in my room. A nice merlot. Does that sound good?"

"It does. How about I meet you out on the porch in about fifteen minutes? I'll bring the glasses."

She hurried to finish her task and popped up

to her room for a moment. She ran a brush through her hair and took a quick look in the mirror. It was hard to disguise the slight blush on her cheeks. She tried to convince herself it was just from the chores and running up the stairs to her room. But her heart laughed at her.

She headed back downstairs to the kitchen. "Gran, I'm going to sit out with Brent for a bit." She reached into the cabinet for two wine glasses.

"Good. You should take a break. You've been working hard all day."

She crossed through the house to the porch and slipped outside. Brent was already there, waiting for her at the far end of the porch. She walked over and sat down, setting the glasses on the table between them.

"I'm dying to know what you found out."

"Here. Just let me pour the wine, then I'll tell you."

He poured the wine and handed her a glass. Their fingers brushed lightly. He paused and looked into her eyes, holding her gaze for a moment longer than necessary. A flicker of something passed between them—a spark of connection. Her heart skipped a beat.

He recovered and held up his glass. "A toast.

To Magnolia Key and the secrets it holds. And to us figuring them out."

She clinked her glass against his. "To uncovering the mysteries of the past."

They both took a sip of the smooth, rich wine. He leaned back in his chair, his eyes still on her. "So, I found some interesting things in Dale's records. Apparently, Prince Lawrence visited Magnolia Key several times in the 1920s, always staying at the Magnolia Landing Boardinghouse."

"Really? I wonder what drew him to the island so often."

"That's the mystery, isn't it? A prince from a small country, regularly visiting a tiny island off the coast of Florida. And it looks like he came at least every other year. There has to be a story there."

She nodded. "There does."

"So I did some digging around about these sister islands that they had back then. Usually, it looked like there would be one big ceremonial meeting when they were declared sister islands and that was about it. But Lawrence kept coming back, repeatedly."

"There has to be some reason." She frowned.

"Or some person…"

"You think he was involved with someone here on the island?"

"Maybe? Just one of the thoughts I had."

Her mind spun with possibilities. "And the way Miss Eleanor reacted when we mentioned his name… She definitely knows something."

"I think so too. I think we need to dig deeper into the prince's connection to the Whitmore family. There's a piece of the puzzle we're missing."

She took another sip of wine, savoring the way it warmed her from the inside out. Or maybe that was the effect of Brent's presence, the intensity of his gaze, the low timbre of his voice as he talked about his findings.

She wanted to spend more time with him. Get to know him better. And she did want to figure out the mysterious Prince Lawrence. She did. "So, tomorrow we'll do more research?"

"I told Dale I thought I'd be back again tomorrow to do more digging. You want to come with me?"

"I do. I'll just need to help Gran with breakfast first, but then I'm all yours." The words slipped out before she could stop them, and she felt her cheeks flush.

His lips quirked up in a smile. "I like the sound of that."

The air between them felt charged, electric. Her heart pounded as she met his gaze, saw the warmth in his eyes. She knew they were treading on dangerous ground, blurring the lines between professional collaboration and personal connection. But at this point, she didn't care. She just enjoyed being with him.

Her breath caught in her throat as he reached over and took her hand in his. His touch was warm and gentle, sending a tingling sensation up her arm. She gazed at him, her heart pounding as he brushed back a lock of her hair that had fallen across her face.

Time seemed to slow down as their eyes met. She found herself lost in the depths of his gaze, noticing the flecks of gold in his brown eyes. The air between them crackled with anticipation. She was almost certain he was going to lean in and kiss her. Part of her desperately wanted him to, while another part felt a nervous warning. She hadn't figured out her own life and what she wanted, much less adding another person to the mix. Her thoughts jumbled around in her mind.

His hand lingered near her face, his thumb

lightly caressing her cheek. She felt herself leaning slightly toward him, drawn by an invisible force. The porch, the B&B, and even the entire island seemed to fade away, leaving just the two of them in this moment.

Just as she thought he might close the distance between them, the porch door creaked open. Gran's voice broke through the silence, shattering the intimate moment.

"Felicity, dear, I was wondering if you could —oh!" Gran stopped short as she stepped onto the porch, taking in the scene before her.

She and Brent quickly pulled apart. Her cheeks burned, and she knew they must be bright red. She glanced at Brent, who looked equally embarrassed, running a hand through his hair and clearing his throat.

"I'm sorry, I didn't mean to interrupt," Gran said, a knowing smile playing at the corners of her mouth.

Felicity stood up, smoothing down her clothes and struggling to keep her voice steady. "You didn't interrupt anything, Gran. We were just... discussing our research findings." The words sounded hollow even to her own ears.

Gran's eyes twinkled with amusement. "Of course, dear. Well, when you're finished with your… *research discussion*, could you help me with something in the kitchen?"

"Sure, Gran. I'll be right there," she replied, still struggling to keep her voice level.

As Gran turned to go back inside, she caught the hint of a smile on her grandmother's face. She knew Gran wasn't fooled for a second.

She turned back to Brent, unsure of what to say. The moment that had been building between them had evaporated, leaving an awkward silence in its wake.

"I… uh… I should go help Gran."

He nodded and rose from his chair. "You should."

"I guess I'll see you tomorrow after breakfast and we'll go do Dale's?"

"I'll see you then."

She turned and fled back inside, not sure if she was glad the moment was interrupted so she had time to figure out her feelings—or if she wished they had just jumped into the kiss and saw where it led them.

That is, if he really had been ready to kiss her.

He had been, hadn't he?

Felicity walked into the kitchen, her heart still somersaulting from the almost-kiss with Brent on the porch. She took a deep breath, trying to calm herself as she approached Gran, who was busy measuring ingredients for her renowned lemon bars.

Gran looked up as she entered, a knowing twinkle in her eyes. "I'm sorry for interrupting. I didn't realize you and Brent were having a moment."

She felt her cheeks flush. "It's okay, Gran. To be honest, I'm not sure what I want these days. My career, my future. It's just all up in the air. It's not fair to drag anyone else into my mess."

Gran put down her mixing bowl and turned to face Felicity, her expression softening. "Oh, honey. I know you've been going through a tough time. Trying to figure out what's next for you. But maybe you just need to give it time. Things have a way of sorting themselves out if you give them time."

She sighed, resting a hip against the counter. "I wish I had your confidence, Gran. I feel so lost right now. Like I don't even know who I am anymore. Teaching used to be everything to me, but now..." she trailed off, shaking her head.

Gran reached out and patted her hand. "You're still the same wonderful, caring person you've always been. Just because you're not sure about your career doesn't mean you've lost yourself. You are more than just a teacher. You're a wonderful woman in your own right. Even without identifying as a teacher. And as for Brent, well, sometimes the best things come along when we least expect them."

She smiled at her grandmother's wisdom. "I do enjoy spending time with him. But I don't want to start something when I'm not sure what I want for myself."

"That's understandable. But don't be afraid to open your heart to the possibilities. You never know where they might lead you." Gran gave her a reassuring smile before turning back to her baking.

She nodded, mulling over her grandmother's words. Gran had a point. She needed to focus on figuring out her own path, but she couldn't deny the growing connection she felt with Brent. His warm brown eyes and easy smile flashed through her mind. Maybe Gran was right. Maybe she just needed to give it time and see where things led, without putting too much pressure on herself or the situation.

Felicity rolled up her sleeves and joined Gran at the kitchen counter, breathing in the scent of the tart lemon. She picked up a wooden spoon and began stirring a bowl of batter. Gran looked up from her work and smiled at her, flour dusting her cheek. "I always say the best place to do your thinking is in the kitchen." She nodded, her eyes sparkling. "Something about the rhythm of baking just helps clear the mind."

She grinned at her grandmother. "I thought you always say that the rhythm of knitting clears your mind."

Gran laughed. "That, too."

CHAPTER 13

The next morning, Felicity headed downstairs to help Gran with breakfast. And if she happened to see Brent too, so much the better. The scent of yeast and cinnamon surrounded her as she hurried down the stairs. Smelled like Gran's cinnamon rolls.

When she entered the kitchen, Gran was pulling out a fresh batch of rolls. She'd been right. "Morning, Gran."

"Morning, sweetheart. Did you sleep well?"

"I did. But no matter how early I get up, you're always up before me." She went over and kissed Gran's cheek.

"Years of running a B&B. The mornings are my busiest time."

She grabbed an apron and started helping

Gran ice the cinnamon rolls. They worked side by side like they had so many times before. The familiarity of the routine soothed her. She could get used to this.

"Oh, Gran. I forgot to tell you last night, Brent found out more information about Prince Lawrence. It seems he came to the island regularly. Then he did some research into the whole sister island thing that some of the islands had going on back then. Regular visits were unusual. There was usually just one big ceremonial gathering. Brent thinks maybe Lawrence kept coming back to visit someone. Maybe he was involved with someone here on the island?"

Gran's expression was unreadable as she paused, the frosting knife hovering over a roll.

"What's wrong, Gran?"

"Nothing, dear. It was all so long ago. I'm sure it doesn't matter much now." Gran's tone was slightly dismissive, but there was a hint of something else beneath the surface.

She frowned. This wasn't like Gran at all. Usually, she loved to talk about the island's history. "I thought you enjoyed learning about Magnolia Key's past as much as I do."

Gran sighed, setting down her knife. "I do.

It's just… sometimes the past is better left where it is."

"But don't you think it's strange? A prince from some tiny country visiting our little island so often?" She pressed, her curiosity aroused by Gran's reluctance.

"People have their reasons for the things they do. Maybe he just really liked it here." Gran's words sounded convincing, but her eyes told a different story.

She knew her grandmother well enough to recognize when she was holding something back. "Gran, if you know something about Prince Lawrence and his visits, you can tell me. I promise I won't share it with anyone, not even Brent, if you don't want me to."

Gran hesitated, clearly torn. She opened her mouth as if to speak, then closed it again, shaking her head. "It's not my story to tell. Please, just let it be."

She wanted to push further, but the pleading look in Gran's eyes stopped her. She nodded slowly, respecting her grandmother's wishes. "All right, Gran. I won't ask again."

"Thank you, dear." Gran's shoulders relaxed, and she picked up her frosting knife once more. "Now, let's finish these rolls before our guests wake up, hmm?"

She followed suit, but her mind was bursting with thoughts. What could Gran possibly know about Prince Lawrence that she didn't want to share? And why did she seem so uncomfortable talking about it? It wasn't like Gran to hide something from her.

As they worked in silence, she couldn't shake the feeling that there was more to this story than met the eye. She glanced at Gran, noticing the faraway look in her eyes, as if she were remembering something from long ago.

Felicity's curiosity burned, but she had to respect Gran's wishes. Still, she wondered about the mysterious prince who had once walked these very same halls of the Bayside Bed and Breakfast.

After breakfast, Felicity met up with Brent. She wanted to tell him about how Gran was acting strangely this morning, but she thought that was an invasion of Gran's privacy. Although she hated keeping anything from Brent. Especially something about the very prince they were looking into. What could Gran possibly know about something that happened before she was even born?

"You ready to head to Dale's?" Brent asked, picking up his satchel stuffed full of his research.

But now, she didn't know how she felt about researching Lawrence. Especially if Gran thought it was a secret that should stay in the past. But she'd promised Brent she would help him. "Yes, I'm ready. Let's go."

They strolled down the sidewalk toward Second Finds, their footsteps in sync. The morning sun warmed her face as a gentle breeze carried the scent of salt and blooming flowers. Her mind churned with conflicting thoughts about their research and Gran's.

"You're awfully quiet this morning," he said, glancing at her with a concerned look. "Everything okay?"

She forced a smile. "Just thinking about what we might find today." And Gran's strange reaction this morning. But she didn't tell him that.

As they walked, her gaze wandered over the familiar storefronts. The hardware store where she'd bought a bicycle bell for her first bike. Gran had patiently taught her to ride until finally, one day, she'd mastered it and taken off, flying down the driveway of the B&B. And there was the ice cream parlor where she and Gran had gotten countless ice cream cones and consumed them walking along the boardwalk. Each place held a memory, tying her to this island in ways she was only now beginning to appreciate.

Brent's voice pulled her from her reverie. "I was thinking we could focus on the years between 1922 and 1928 today. That seems to be when Prince Lawrence's visits were most frequent."

She nodded, still uncertain about this whole research into the prince.

They rounded the corner, and Second Finds came into view. Colorful flags fluttered out front, advertising antiques and local history.

Brent held the door open for her. The familiar scent of old books and polished wood surrounded them. Dale looked up from behind the counter, his face lighting up with a warm smile.

"Well, if it isn't my favorite historical detectives," he said, setting aside the book he'd been reading. "Back for more clues about our mysterious prince?"

She felt a stab of guilt. Should she even be pursuing this if Gran seemed uncomfortable with it? But Brent's enthusiasm was infectious, and she found herself nodding along.

"I'm glad you're here again. I found another box with photos from that era, and I put it on the table in the back room."

"Thanks."

They headed toward the back room and settled at the table. Brent opened the book and started looking through the photos, flipping each one over to see if anything was written on the backs.

She reached in to get a batch of photos and found an old book. She pulled it out, trailing her finger along the spine. "Look at this." The faded book was titled *Magnolia Key: A History in Pictures*.

As she opened the book, a loose photograph fluttered to the floor. She bent to retrieve it and turned it over. There on the back in scrolling penmanship someone had written: Prince Lawrence's third visit.

Brent leaned over closer to her. "His third visit, huh? I wonder just how many times he came to visit. And when he stopped coming so often."

"You'd think a prince would be busy back in his own country, wouldn't you?"

"Maybe he became king of his country? Too busy to come back? I still think my idea that he was interested in some woman here on the island was why he kept returning. Of course, that's just a wild guess, but it makes sense."

And that also made sense that Gran knew something about it and didn't want the secret to come out. But why? And who?

Dale walked into the room. "Any luck finding anything else?"

"We found a photo of Lawrence. It says it was from his third visit," she said, handing Dale the photo.

"Oh, that reminds me," Brent said as he opened his satchel and pulled out a photo. "I have this old photo of my mother. I have no idea where she was, but there is a lighthouse in the background. Haven't had time to really research it, but I did find out her family was from this area originally." He handed it to Dale.

Dale took a close look at it and a smile spread across his face. "Yep, I sure can identify this lighthouse. It's our lighthouse here on the island. Or it was. I've seen old photos of it. A storm came in and damaged it, and it was rebuilt stronger, so it no longer looks like this. But it's ours. Let me find you a photo."

Dale walked over to a shelf, pulled out a box, and brought over a handful of photos, handing them to Brent.

Brent's eyes widened as he looked through them. "It is the same lighthouse. I can't believe my mother was here on this very island. I wonder if she was just visiting. Or do you think she might have even lived here?"

"I don't know." Dale grinned. "Looks like you've got yourself even more research to do."

Felicity and Brent headed back to the B&B. Townspeople smiled or nodded at them as they passed. The once-again familiar sights of the town slipped past them as they slowly strolled along the sidewalk. Brent was quiet as they walked along.

Finally, she looked over at him. "So, your mother. She might have lived here on Magnolia Key. That's really something."

He nodded, a thoughtful look on his face. "It's possible. From what Dale said, that photo I found with the lighthouse in the background is definitely from Magnolia Key."

"But you're not sure if she actually lived here, right?"

"No, I'm not. No one in my family ever

mentioned it, but then again, they didn't talk about her much." He paused and frowned. "So it doesn't give me a definitive clue. It could have simply been a vacation. Magnolia Key was a popular spot back then."

She stopped beside him. "The island still is."

"I'll have to look into it more. See if I can find any records that prove she lived here. Or prove she didn't live here. But at least it's a start."

They continued walking and reached the B&B, its wide porch welcoming them back. Without discussing it, they both headed for the porch swing. She settled in, feeling the familiar creak of the chains as Brent sat beside her.

"What was your mother like?" she asked, genuinely curious.

A soft smile curved his lips. "From what I can remember—and it's not much—she was vibrant. Always laughing, always ready for an adventure. But there was a sadness to her sometimes. Though maybe I'm remembering that from when she was ill. Like I said, my memories of her are few and kind of jumbled."

"It might be nice to figure out where she grew up. Learn some more about her. Maybe it would make you feel more connected to her."

She grinned at him. "And we all know how you love to research."

He laughed. "I do. And I think it might help to find out more about her if I can."

They fell into a comfortable silence, the rhythmic creaking of the porch swing accompanying their thoughts. She glanced over and studied his profile, noticing the set of his jaw and the intensity in his eyes as he gazed out at the horizon.

"What if you do find out she lived here?" she asked softly. "What would that mean for you?"

He turned to look at her, his brown eyes meeting hers. "I'm not sure. But I think I'd be glad. Glad to have a connection to this place. A connection… anywhere."

She nodded, understanding. She felt the same way about Magnolia Key, about the roots her family had put down here. It was comforting and grounding.

"We'll figure it out," she said, surprising herself with the term *we*, but it felt right.

He smiled a warm, genuine smile that made her heart skip a beat. "Thank you," he said simply.

That heart-skipping thing and the way she

felt when she spent time with him confused her. Of course, everything confused her these days.

They sat and moved slowly, back and forth on the swing, until finally, she turned to him, daring to ask the question that had been on her mind all day. "Can I ask you something?"

"Of course. Anything." He turned to look at her.

"You were going to kiss me, weren't you? Last night before Gran interrupted."

He grinned. "I was. Did you want me to?"

She turned and looked out at the bay for a moment, gathering her thoughts. "I… I honestly don't know. I'm not sure now is a good time for a relationship. I'm so confused about so much in my life. My identity is wrapped up in being a teacher and now the thought of going back just… leaves me feeling empty." She looked up into his eyes and took a deep breath. "Can we just be friends? Is that okay with you? Besides, we're both leaving soon. It seems fruitless to start something that can't go anywhere."

He locked his gaze with hers, a sadness hovering about his features. "I understand how you feel. I know you have things to sort out. But

I won't say I'm not disappointed. I felt… something. I thought you might too."

She looked down at her hands, breaking their contact. "I just don't know how I feel about anything right now. My life. Anything. It's not the right time to start something, I don't think."

"If that's what you need, I'll back off. We can stay friends. Research partners. That's fine." His voice almost sounded like he was telling the truth.

She glanced up, relieved to find that his look said he understood. That he was fine with her decision. She let out a long breath and smiled at him. "Good, I'm glad that's settled."

Brent stood. "I think I'm going to go for a walk on the beach. Been inside a lot doing all this research."

She rose. "And I should go in and see if I can help Gran. That's why I came here this summer, after all." To help Gran and sort things out. Only… things just kept getting more and more complicated. At least he was supportive of her decision. They should just be friends.

"Okay, I'll see you tomorrow." Brent turned and headed down the stairs.

She leaned against the porch railing, staring

out at the bay. The ferry was barely visible in the distance, bringing another load of people to the island just like it had brought her at the beginning of the summer.

This summer had not been like she'd imagined it would be. But the slower pace and helping Gran was such a welcomed change from teaching. Maybe by the end of the summer, she'd be ready to head back to her job, recharged and ready to go.

Maybe.

And now that she'd talked things out with Brent, that was settled too.

Maybe.

Brent walked along the beach, his feet sinking into the soft sand with each step. The sound of the waves crashing against the shore filled his ears, and the light breeze blew through his hair. But his thoughts were on Felicity and their talk.

She'd made it clear that it wasn't the right time for a relationship. Maybe she was right, but he couldn't deny his disappointment. He'd been ready to see where things were heading between them. Over the past few weeks, he'd grown to like her more and more. Her passion for uncovering the island's history, her kindness, and her warm smile had drawn him in.

But he had to respect her decision. She was going through a lot, trying to figure out her career and find contentment in her work again. He understood that she needed to sort that out before considering anything else. Still, a part of him wished they could be more than just friends.

And he felt like she'd pulled back on wanting to research the prince. He wasn't sure what that was about. Although she had said she'd help him research his mother.

His mother.

How strange to think she'd visited this very same island, and walked these very same beaches. He couldn't wait to dig in and research more. He had this burning need to find out more about her. About her childhood. Her family. Any and every little detail.

As he continued his walk, he found himself approaching the lighthouse. The tall structure rose up against the blue sky. He paused and stared at it, then realized he was standing in almost the exact same place his mother had been standing in the photograph. A sense of connection flowed through him. A peace along with the longing to know more.

He climbed the steps leading up to the base of the lighthouse and stood where surely his mother had once been. The view was breathtaking, the vast expanse of the ocean stretching out before him. He wondered what had brought his mother to Magnolia Key all those years ago.

"Hey, Mom. I'm right here. Right where you've been before. Walking the same beach. I wish… I wish I had gotten the chance to know you better."

Sadness swept through him for his loss. For the years he didn't get to spend with her. For the loneliness that had been his life growing up without her.

A seagull swooped overhead, turned, and swooped back by him, coming to land at the edge of the foamy waves. It turned and looked at him, then scurried down the beach before soaring up in the sky.

He leaned against the railing, letting the warm sun wash over his face. Despite the disappointment of Felicity's decision, peace settled over him just being here. The island had a funny way of soothing him, and he was grateful for the opportunity to explore its history and his own family's connection to it.

He knew he needed to focus on his research and the book he was writing. That had been his goal from the start, and he couldn't let his feelings for Felicity distract him from that. And he didn't really even know what his feelings were because she didn't want to explore them.

He would continue to work with her, enjoy her company, and enjoy the friendship they had formed. Maybe, in time, things would change, but for now, he had to accept what was.

With a deep breath, he turned away from the lighthouse and started making his way back along the beach. As he walked, determination crept through him, taking a firm hold. He would uncover the secrets of Magnolia Key and his mother's past, and he would do it with Felicity or without her. He promised himself that he'd uncover the prince's secrets and find out everything he could about his mother.

Felicity sat in her room that night, knitting on the scarf she'd started at the knitting club. She really should make some progress on it to show to the ladies at the next meeting. Although, if she were being honest, she was hiding out in her room, not wanting to run into Brent again tonight. She just needed some time to think. And give him some time to think.

A knock sounded at her door, and for a brief moment, she hoped it was Brent. *What? That didn't make any sense. She was avoiding him, remember?*

"Honey, it's Gran."

"Come in."

Gran came into the room, carrying a tray with tea and her knitting bag slung over one shoulder. "I made us some chamomile tea. You were quiet at dinner. I thought you might want to talk?"

"Gran, I'm supposed to be helping you. You're not supposed to be waiting on me."

"I'll never quit spoiling you, dear. It's what grandmothers do."

She got up and took the tray from Gran, setting it on the small table. "Sit then, and have some with me."

Gran smiled. "I was hoping you'd say that."

They settled into the comfortable chairs by the window with their tea, and Gran picked up her knitting. "So, is something bothering you?"

"No. Not really. I just had a talk with Brent.

Told him it was the wrong time to get involved with someone."

"And what did he say?"

"That it was fine with him. That we could be just friends."

"And did you believe him?" Gran raised an eyebrow.

"I…" She set down her cup and sighed. "I kind of believed him. I think he was disappointed with my choice. But he said it would be fine. We can be friends. Research partners."

"And that's what you want?"

"I think so." She shrugged. "Of course, I don't really know what I want anymore."

"Seems a shame to shut that door before you even know what might happen."

"Maybe. But I think it's the smart thing to do."

"Sometimes the smart thing to do and what our heart wants are two different things."

Gran always had wise words. She shook her head and changed the subject. "Oh, and we got sidetracked from researching the prince." She guessed Gran would be glad about that, at least. "We discovered that a photo Brent found of his mother was of her standing here on Magnolia

Key as a young girl. I didn't recognize it because it had the old lighthouse in the background. You know, before it was rebuilt."

"That was a long time ago when the storm damaged it. I think it's been rebuilt once and remodeled once." Gran paused and took a sip of her tea. "So Brent thinks his mother visited here?"

"Maybe. Or possibly even lived here. He's going to research it."

"I hope he can find out more about her."

"I do too. I think it will help him feel closer to her. I think he had a pretty bleak childhood. Passed around from relative to relative. His dad worked overseas a lot."

"That's too bad. A child should always feel secure and know they have a home."

"I think he's hoping he's connected to Magnolia Key. For his sake, I hope he is too." She smiled. "It's nice being connected to this island."

"The island does something to you, doesn't it? Claims a part of your heart." Gran picked up her knitting. "Now, show me your scarf."

She showed Gran her progress, and they chatted and knitted while they sipped their tea. She couldn't ask for a better way to spend an evening. Well, maybe if she'd sort out what she was going to do with her life, it would be a bit more peaceful.

Gran looked up and smiled at her. "Don't worry. You'll figure things out."

Her grandmother always did know what she was thinking.

CHAPTER 15

Brent didn't actually sneak out of the B&B the next morning, but he did stealthily go downstairs and slip out the door, careful not to catch the attention of anyone having—or serving—breakfast. He headed to Coastal Coffee for breakfast instead. He wasn't quite up to friendly chatting with Felicity.

The morning sun was just beginning to warm the air, and sunbeams flickered through the palm fronds. Walking these streets had become a familiar routine to him, a comforting routine he enjoyed. He reached Coastal Coffee and slipped inside. Beverly waved to him and called out, "Sit anywhere you like. Be with you in a sec."

He took a seat near the back of the cafe. No

use sitting in the window where he could be seen if Felicity happened to walk by. Okay, now he was just being ridiculous.

Beverly came over and placed a mug on the table. "Coffee?"

"Please."

"Darlene run out of breakfast this morning?" Beverly grinned.

He laughed. "I just had some work to do in town this morning and thought I'd stop by here and grab a quick breakfast for a change." He figured that was a better answer than admitting he was hiding out.

Beverly nodded toward the chalkboard. "We have cinnamon rolls today. And Sal—that's our cook—made some spinach quiche."

"I'll have the quiche with a side of hash browns."

"Good choice. Won't be long." Beverly headed the kitchen, and he opened a folder he brought with him. He leafed through the printouts until he came to the photo of his mother.

He stared at it, tracing the outline of her with his finger. The lighthouse rose behind her, gleaming in the sunlight. His mother's smile was soft, almost shy, as she gazed at the camera. She couldn't have been more than a teenager in the picture.

He wondered what she had been like back then. Was she outgoing or reserved? Did she love the beach as much as he did? What dreams did she have for her future?

He tried to remember her voice, her laugh, but those memories were long faded. What would it have been like to know her back then, as a young woman, full of life and possibility?

His eyes drifted to her dress in the photo. The colors were faded. He realized with a twinge of regret that he didn't even know her favorite color. Such a simple thing, and yet it was lost to him forever.

What foods did she love? Did she have a sweet tooth like him? He remembered her making pot roast on Sundays, but was that her favorite, or just something she knew he and his dad enjoyed?

His chest tightened as he thought about how young she was when she died. There were so many conversations they never got to have, so many experiences they'd missed out on sharing.

He imagined what life might have been like if she'd lived. Would she have encouraged his interest in history? Would she have shared stories about her time on Magnolia Key? Maybe she would have come with him on this research trip, pointing out places she remembered from her youth.

He sighed. His entire life would have been different if she had lived. He might have chosen a different career path, lived in a different city. He might have been a different person entirely.

But then, he realized, he might never have come to Magnolia Key. Never met Felicity. Never uncovered this mystery that seemed to tie his family to this place.

Beverly came over, interrupting his thoughts. She placed his food on the table and nodded toward the photo in his hand. "Who's that? Part of your research?"

"It's my mother." He handed the photo to her.

"She's pretty."

"That's taken right here on the island."

Beverly looked at the photo closely. "Oh, it is. With the old lighthouse before it got rebuilt. And we've recently had some restoration work done on it too. Looks very different now from what it looks like in this photo."

"Dale pointed out to me that the photo was

taken here. He recognized the old version of the lighthouse."

"So your mom visited here too? Or lived here?"

"I'm not sure. I did a little research online last night, but can't find any record of her family here on Magnolia Key."

Beverly pursed her lips, her brow creasing. "You know. You should show that to Miss Eleanor. She might know. The Whitmores know everyone on the island. Their family has been here for generations." Beverly tilted her head to a table further back in the cafe. "She's over there having her breakfast if you want to show it to her."

He glanced over. "I'll eat and let her finish her meal, then I'll pop over there and show it to her." He had to admit he was a bit intimidated by the idea. She'd been very vague about Prince Lawrence, though he was sure she'd recognized the name. But maybe she would know something about his mother? He couldn't let the opportunity to ask her pass by.

He ate his meal, keeping an eye on Miss Eleanor. He wanted to catch her before she left. As she appeared to be finishing her coffee, he rose and crossed over to her table.

She looked up at him pointedly. "Yes?"

"Good morning, Miss Eleanor. Brent Dunn, remember me?"

"Yes, of course." She nodded brusquely.

"I wanted to show you this photograph and see if you recognized the woman in it."

Miss Eleanor just sat there, not extending a hand nor agreeing to look at it. He held the photo out to her. "Please? Can you just see if you recognize her?"

She slowly took the photo, and the color drained out of her features. A small gasp escaped her lips. "Joanie," she said softly, almost as if she didn't know she said the word out loud.

He steadied himself against the table. "Yes. Joan. Her maiden name was—"

"Burton." She looked up at him, her eyes darkening. "Where did you get this?"

"I found it in my mother's things. It's... my mother."

He swore she got even paler. "Your mother?"

He nodded.

She traced her finger along the edge of the photo, almost as if she were remembering the exact moment it was taken, before looking back up at him. "And is she—alive?"

He shook his head. "No, she died when I was a child."

"I see."

"Did you know her?" he asked as he took the seat across from her.

"I did. I knew… her brother."

"My mother had a brother?" Why had no one ever said that to him? Of course, his father's family had raised him and didn't talk about his mother. Maybe they didn't even know much about her.

"Yes. Jonah."

Miss Eleanor's voice cracked.

"I never heard anything about Mom having a brother."

Miss Eleanor looked at him, and he knew what he was seeing in her eyes was raw pain. "Jonah… he died. During a hurricane that came through. He was working on securing boats at the marina and was swept away. I never saw Joanie again after the hurricane. After Jonah was… gone."

He felt a stab of pain for the loss of an uncle he never even knew existed. "Did they live here on the island?" He struggled to process all the information Miss Eleanor was giving him.

"No, they lived on the mainland. But Jonah

worked here on the island. Came over on his boat every day. He often brought Joanie with him. She adored him. She was about four years younger, I believe. But every summer, she came over with him while he worked and hung out at the marina with him." She tapped her finger on the photo. "I was there that day the photo was taken. One of Joanie. One of Jonah."

"I only found the one of my mother." He frowned. "What about their parents? Do you know anything about them?"

Miss Eleanor gave a small smile. "They were hardworking people. Your grandfather worked as a carpenter. Mostly on the mainland, but sometimes over here on the island. I believe your grandmother was a seamstress."

"Well, that gives me a little more to go on. I'm trying to learn more about my mother's side of the family. You've been a big help."

She nodded slowly, a sadness clinging to her features. "I hope you find what you're looking for."

He rose. "I hope so too."

Felicity cleared up the last of the breakfast dishes and brought a tray full of them into the kitchen. She'd been sorry that Brent hadn't shown up for breakfast this morning. But then, she'd been a little relieved too.

"Here you go, Gran. Last of the dishes." She set the tray on the counter. "Why don't you let me finish cleaning up here?"

"Nonsense. I can get these. Don't you want to find Brent and help him with his research?"

"I thought I'd work on the storage shed today. Go through the boxes and clean up in there. I'm sure there are things we don't need anymore. If I get it cleaned up, you'll have more storage space for things we do need."

"You don't have to do that. That's quite a project."

"Gran, I'm here to help, remember?"

"Okay, okay. But don't overdo it. You don't have to tackle it all today."

Felicity crossed the yard and pulled open the door to the storage shed, a musty scent greeting her. Dust danced in the beams of morning light that slipped through the windows, adding an otherworldly quality to the cluttered interior.

She glanced over to the corner where she used to play as a young girl. Believing this was her castle, and the world outside, her kingdom. The memories brought a smile to her lips.

She stepped farther inside, eyeing the stacks of boxes piled against the walls. Some sat haphazardly, while others were neatly labeled in Gran's careful handwriting.

She'd always found it fascinating how a single shed could hold so many memories. She explored every corner of the space as a child, building imaginary worlds out of forgotten treasures. Now, as an adult, the shed represented a different kind of adventure—one rooted in practicality and the desire to assist Gran.

After clearing space on the floor, she set to work, rifling through the first box of red, white, and blue decorations—remnants of Fourth of July celebrations. The next box held odd kitchenware. Each box told a story of the guests who'd once stayed at Bayside, of summer flings and lazy afternoons spent on the porch. She fondly remembered one particular family who returned every summer while their children were young, and she always shared her special place here in the shed with their daughters.

Enough of the memories. She had a job to do. She divided the contents into two sections. Items to keep and items to discard. A stray glass vase, pretty but with a small chip at the rim, joined the pile meant for charitable donation. The Christmas lights with frayed cords went into the trash pile. An antique lamp that didn't work, but look liked it might be of some value, was set aside to show to Dale. Maybe he could fix it.

Despite the physical exertion, she found comfort in the repetitive task. Her mind wandered to other simpler times, before the complications of adulthood overtook her dreams. As she worked, she thought about Brent and his recent findings—his mother's connection to Magnolia Key, the tangled history and secrets they'd uncovered about the prince, and the whirlwind it had stirred within her.

After sorting through what must have been the twentieth box, she hauled it to the porch, setting it down with a gratifying thump.

And there he was—Brent—sauntering down the path leading back to the B&B. He was backlit by the sun and looking as if he belonged to the landscape itself. His steps were even, yet there was something about his unhurried gait that highlighted his growing connection with the island.

She hesitated for a moment, caught between

impulse and indecision. Should she call out to him? Part of her wanted to, eager to pick up their conversation where they'd left off, to hear more about what he'd discovered. Perhaps he'd made progress on his mother's history, or located another piece in the puzzle of Prince Lawrence. Yet another part of her balked, wary of tangling further with emotions she'd carefully compartmentalized.

So there she stood, gripping the box, with invisible strings pulling her in conflicting directions.

He seemed unaware of her presence, absorbed in his own thoughts. She watched him for a moment longer, admiring his relaxed presence while she stood there as tense as a fiddle string.

A fragile balance settled on her, warring between wanting to reach out and allowing things to remain unsaid. The presence of her uncertainty felt like a physical weight. She knew it wasn't just about speaking to him right now. It was about everything she'd been feeling. Her desire for change, the pull back toward the island—a familiar place of comfort and security —and her indecision about her future.

Seconds ticked by, yet it felt like an eternity.

Then the decision was taken out of her hands. He spied her and waved, turning to cross the distance to the shed.

Her heartbeat quickened as Brent approached, his tentative smile disarming her defenses. She busied herself with the box, attempting to appear nonchalant.

"Hey there. What are you up to?" He said it normally. Just like their conversation last night had never happened. Like he fully grasped the whole let's-just-be-friends-thing and was fine with it. And she didn't know if that made her happy—or not.

She gestured to the shed. "Just cleaning out some of the old stuff. Trying to make more space for Gran." She refused to admit she was hiding out…

"Well, I have some news." He stepped up on the porch and leaned against the railing, a mere foot or so away from her.

"Oh?" She forced her gaze away from the few inches of railing between them.

"I went to Coastal Coffee this morning and ran into Miss Eleanor. She recognized my mother in the photo I showed her."

Surprise swept through her. "Really? What did she say?"

"Apparently, my mother didn't live on the island, but on the mainland. But Miss Eleanor knew her. And her brother, Jonah. But Jonah died in a hurricane."

"Oh, I'm sorry."

He gave her a small smile. "It's okay. I didn't even know he existed. I mean, it's sad, but it's also another piece of the puzzle, you know? I have more to go on now, to research my mom's family."

She was a tiny bit disappointed she hadn't been there with him when he found out this new information. She ignored that feeling and smiled at him. "That's great that you have more to go on now. It must be kind of exciting to uncover these new pieces of your family history."

"It really is. I feel like I'm getting closer to understanding my mom's connection to this place."

She was genuinely happy for him. "So, what's your next step?"

"I'm going to do some digging into records about Jonah and see if I can find any information about the hurricane he died in. Maybe that will lead me to more about my mom's time here."

She felt a familiar tug of curiosity, wanting

to offer her help, but she held back. They'd agreed to just be friends, and she didn't want to complicate things further.

"Well, good luck with your research," she said, lifting a box and moving it to a different pile—the wrong pile—she'd just have to move it back when he left. "I should probably get back to this."

He straightened up from the railing. "Right, of course. I'll let you get back to it. Thanks for listening."

He turned and started walking back toward the B&B. A mix of emotions swirled inside her as she watched him go—relief that their interaction had been friendly and uncomplicated, but also a twinge of disappointment that he hadn't asked for her help with his research.

As he climbed onto the porch of the B&B, she found herself rooted to the spot, unable to tear her eyes away.

She stood there a moment longer, then turned and picked up the box to move it back to the correct pile. The weight of the box in her arms served as an anchor to reality while her thoughts drifted between what could be and what should be. The gentle island breeze rustled the leaves of the magnolia beside the shed, seeming to whisper about the lost possibilities she wasn't quite ready to acknowledge were gone for good.

Eleanor sat at her dressing table, the same one she'd had since childhood. The antique wood was worn smooth from decades of use, its surface laden with an array of brushes, lotions, and face creams. She picked up her silver-handled hairbrush and began to stroke her hair, the rhythmic motion soothing her troubled thoughts.

At her feet, Winston snoozed contentedly. His soft snores provided a reassuring background noise as she continued her nightly ritual.

She set down her hairbrush and stared at the side drawer, trying to make up her mind. The drawer called to her, and she slowly opened it, not sure if she was making the right decision. Her fingers searched the back until she felt the edge of the envelope. She hesitated for a moment before pulling it out.

Opening the worn, wrinkled envelope, she

slipped out a photograph. It was a picture of Jonah, standing in front of the old Magnolia Key lighthouse. The same lighthouse that appeared in the photograph Brent had found of his mother, Joanie.

Jonah stood there, a wide smile on his face. He'd had such a wonderful smile that never failed to warm her every time she saw it. Back then, all those years ago… and now, to this day. Though now, it brought with it a sadness that seeped through her.

The two photographs—the one of Joanie and the one of Jonah—had been taken on the same day, a day etched in her memory. She'd kept Jonah's photograph hidden away all these years, rarely allowing herself the luxury—and pain—of taking it out and looking at it.

Her eyes traced the familiar lines of Jonah's face, a face she had once known so well. The years had passed, but the memories remained as vivid as ever.

Along with the regrets.

Her fingers trembled slightly as she held the photograph, a reminder of the secrets she'd carried for so long. The secrets wrapped around her, like the heavy fog that sometimes covered the island, surrounding it in a blanket of impenetrable mist.

But now, she glanced away from the smiling man, so full of life and vitality. She just couldn't afford to remember the good times, and the pain was too searing to remember the bad times, some of the darkest days of her life. Days she had to hide her pain from everyone. Her family. Her friends.

No one knew about Jonah, not even Darlene. So this secret, at least, could remain in the past. With a long sigh, she slipped the photograph back into the envelope and returned it to its hiding place. She closed the drawer, sealing away the memories once more.

Winston stirred at her feet, sensing her distress. She reached down and patted his head, finding comfort in his warm, soft fur.

She picked up the face cream and spread it on her face with rote motions as thoughts bounced around her mind. If only Brent wasn't so intent on stirring up the past. But truth be told, she liked Brent in spite of herself. She liked his thoughtfulness. His intelligence. His curiosity. His determination to find out what happened to his mother. She could see little glimpses of Joanie in him.

Maybe his whole quest to find out more about Joanie and his family would lessen his desire to find out more about Prince Lawrence. But she doubted it. Brent didn't seem to be the type to let his research slide.

She could only hope that if the truth about the prince finally came to light, it would not destroy her family's reputation. For now, she would continue to guard the secrets, just as the lighthouse guarded the island's shores.

CHAPTER 16

Felicity helped Gran clean up after breakfast the next day. Brent had come to breakfast this morning and still sat out in the dining room, sipping coffee and looking through one of his constant companion files. She went out to collect another tray of dirty dishes and Gran came out after her, looking around the room.

"I'll get those last dishes. I wondered if you could do me a favor. I thought it might look nice to put up some pinwheels in front of the porch. We're supposed to have a light breeze for the next few days. They'll look cheerful, don't you think?"

"They would." Gran was always trying to make the porch even more inviting. Flags on the

Fourth of July, pumpkins at Halloween, and of course, she went all out for Christmas. But Gran was right, the pinwheels would bring a pop of color to the porch. "Are they in the storage shed?"

"No, I think they're in the house. In the back room."

"I'll go hunt for them."

Gran looked at Brent. "Brent, would you mind helping Felicity? There are so many boxes in storage and I haven't had time to organize them."

She shot Gran a glare, knowing perfectly well what her grandmother was doing. She was trying to get them to spend time together.

"Of course, I'll help." Brent rose and collected his folders. He sent Felicity a quick look as if asking for her approval.

She hesitated momentarily, still feeling awkward around him after their conversation about just being friends. But she pushed those thoughts aside and nodded. "Actually, that would be great. Would appreciate the help."

They made their way to the storage room, an awkward silence stretching between them. She turned on the light, illuminating the cluttered space. "I'm not sure where to start." She looked around the fully packed room.

"I'll start in the back." Brent moved to the far end of the room.

They began shifting boxes, carefully setting them aside as they searched. They fell into a rhythm, working together despite the lingering awkwardness.

As Brent moved a particularly large box, he paused, frowning at the wall behind the shelf. "Hey, come take a look at this. Does something seem off to you?"

She walked over, peering at the section of wall he was staring at. At first glance, it looked normal, but as she studied it, she noticed a slight irregularity in the paneling. There was something odd about the way the wall looked. It was as if it wasn't quite flush with the rest of the surface.

"That's strange." She frowned. "I've never noticed anything unusual about this wall before."

He reached out, running his hand along the surface. Suddenly, there was a soft click, and a small section of the wall sprang open, revealing a hidden compartment.

She gasped. "I had no idea that was there. Gran's never mentioned anything like this."

He carefully reached into the compartment and pulled out a yellowed envelope. "Look at this," he said, his voice filled with excitement. "It's an old letter."

She leaned in, her curiosity piqued. The envelope was addressed simply to "V" in faded, elegant handwriting. She glanced at Brent, seeing her own mix of surprise and intrigue mirrored in his expression.

"V as in Vera?" She asked.

"I don't know. Should we open it?" He turned the envelope over in his hands.

She bit her lip, torn between her curiosity and Gran's warning that they should leave the past in the past. "I'm not sure."

"It's been here a long time. You can tell by the weathered paper. I think we should open it. We might find out something that will help us with our research on Prince Lawrence."

She didn't know how to stop him and didn't know if she wanted to stop him. It surely wouldn't hurt to open the envelope after all this time, would it?

Still hearing Gran's words in her head, she nodded to him. He opened the envelope and pulled out two pages. "Look, it is addressed to Vera."

She peered over his shoulder. "What does it say?"

"Let's move under the light."

They walked under the light, and she read over his shoulder. When they were done reading, she looked at Brent. "This pretty much confirms that Lawrence and Vera were having an affair, doesn't it? He tells her he loves her. He talks about their secret meeting place."

"And that last line. That he'll send word to her when it's the right time for her to see the letter. And if she's reading it, she'll know where he'll meet up with her. He asked her to run away with him. But I guess he never did send word, since the letter is still hidden here."

Gran called from the kitchen. "Felicity? Did you find those pinwheels?"

"Not yet. Still looking," she called out. She turned to Brent. "Let's find those pinwheels."

"Then we can show Darlene the letter."

"I… I don't know if we should."

He looked at her with a confused expression. "Why not?"

"Just… give me time to talk to her first. Can you do that?"

"If that's what you want." He handed her the letter, and she tucked it in her pocket.

They resumed their search as her mind whirled with questions. She guessed Lawrence hid the letter on one of his visits. That was the only logical explanation. But why was it still there? Why had he never sent word to Vera to find the letter?

"Found the pinwheels." Brent interrupted her thoughts and held out a box with pinwheels poking out of the top.

"Great, let's bring them to Gran."

They headed to the kitchen, and she was surprised to see Dale sitting at the table, sipping coffee with Gran.

Brent set the box with the pinwheels on the table and stretched out a hand to Dale. "Morning."

"Good morning. I had a bit of a breakthrough with my research. Found out a bit more about the scandal I remembered reading about."

"You did? What did you find?" Brent sat down across from Dale. Felicity stood near

Gran, noticing the cautious look on her grandmother's face.

"On one of the prince's visits, he had a pendant with him. It went missing, or possibly it was stolen. But I found a photo of the pendant and compared it to the one Tori found hidden in Vera's dressing table at the theater. It's the very same pendant."

She looked over at Brent, sure the same thought was going through his mind. This further confirmed that Lawrence and Vera were having an affair.

"Really?"

"My theory is Lawrence gave it to her. But I did some more research into the prince. The year the pendant went missing is the year he formally became engaged to the woman he married a year later. From what I found out, the two were destined to marry from the first year they were born. An arranged marriage of sorts. Who knew they still did that in the 1920s, but I guess they did. She was some kind of royalty too." Dale set down his cup.

Brent sat looking thoughtful, then spoke. "I wonder if Lawrence and Vera were..." He looked at Gran. "Ah, an item. Maybe they were involved, but then the prince chose his duty and obligation to his country over Vera?"

"Maybe giving her the pendant was his way of saying he was sorry to Vera?" Dale guessed.

"Maybe."

"Or maybe they were just acquaintances. And she found the pendant after he left. We don't really know what happened. And it's not right to make guesses, now is it?" Gran stared at all three of them.

"No, you're right. We don't know anything for certain." Brent looked up, and she saw what he was saying without words. They should show Gran the letter.

Dale rose. "Well, I should head back to the shop. Darlene, thanks for the coffee." He turned to Brent. "Let me know if I can help with any more research."

"I will. You've been very helpful."

Dale left, and Brent stood. "I should go too. I want to do some more research on my mother's family. I'll see you two later." He gave her a meaningful stare before leaving the kitchen.

"Gran, we need to talk."

"There's nothing to talk about. This nonsense about Vera and Lawrence is just gossip and rumors."

"Actually… it's not." She pulled out the letter and handed it to Gran. "We found this in a hidden compartment in the storage room."

Gran took the letter and walked over to where her reading glasses rested on the counter. She slipped them on and slowly unfolded the pages. She read the pages, then set them on the counter, standing quietly for a moment.

"It appears the prince did have feelings for Vera," Gran finally said.

"It does look like that." She took a step closer to Gran. "And he asked her to go away with him."

"But Dale said he was engaged to some woman from royalty and married her."

"It does seem like that happened." She nodded.

"What is Brent going to do with this knowledge?" Gran frowned, eyeing the letter.

"I'm not sure. It is a bit of the island's history. Especially interesting since it involved a prince."

"But surely their private life doesn't need to

be made public," Gran asserted, as if there was no doubt.

"I'm not sure what Brent plans to do."

"He should do the right thing and just let all this go." Gran took off her glasses, handed her back the letter, and strode out of the kitchen.

But she wasn't sure that Brent would agree with Gran's assertion.

CHAPTER 17

Darlene walked down the quiet street toward Eleanor's house, her steps measured and full of purpose. The afternoon sun cast long shadows across the well-manicured lawns of Magnolia Key. As she approached Eleanor's house, she could see her old friend sitting on the front porch, Winston curled up at her feet.

Eleanor looked up as Darlene climbed the steps, a questioning expression on her face. "Darlene, what brings you by this afternoon?"

She settled into the chair next to Eleanor, taking a moment to pat Winston's head. The old dog thumped his tail lazily against the wooden porch.

"We need to talk. I'm afraid I have some

news that might be… unsettling," she began, her voice low and careful.

Eleanor's eyebrows knitted together. "Oh? What's happened?"

"It's about Brent and Felicity's research. They've found something. A letter, actually."

Eleanor's hand tightened on the arm of her chair. "A letter? What kind of letter?"

"It's from Prince Lawrence," she said softly. "To Vera."

Eleanor closed her eyes briefly, her face paling. When she opened them again, there was a mix of resignation and worry in her eyes. "I see. And what did this letter say?"

She hesitated, then continued, "It seems to confirm that the prince had feelings for Vera. Strong feelings. He… he invited her to leave with him."

Eleanor nodded slowly, her lips pressed into a thin line. "I always feared something like this might surface one day. I've always guessed that Vera and Lawrence had an affair from the few remarks I overheard my father say."

"There's more," she added, her voice gentle. "Dale has been doing some digging of his own. He's made a connection between the pendant that went missing during one of Lawrence's visits and the one that Tori found in the dressing table at the theater."

Eleanor's eyes widened, and she shook her head. "Oh, dear. This is… this is not good. Not good at all."

She reached out and touched Eleanor's hand. "I know. I'm worried about what Brent might do with this information. He seems quite determined to uncover every detail about the island's history."

Eleanor sighed heavily, her gaze drifting out to the street. "It was all so long ago. I had hoped… well, I suppose it doesn't matter what I hoped. The past has a way of catching up with us, doesn't it?"

"It usually does." She nodded. "I know the whole prince story would add a bit of spark and interest to his writing about the area. I'm not sure what he plans to do with it."

"He needs to just forget he ever heard about it," Eleanor stated firmly. "There is no good in dragging Vera's name through the mud. Or the Whitmore family's reputation. Surely he can see that."

"Maybe." But she wasn't as certain as her friend. If Brent could find all this out, so could another researcher who was diligent enough. If

Brent published his book on the history of the area and left this information out, and someone came along later and published the information, it could look like Brent wasn't quite the authority he made himself out to be.

"As if it wasn't enough that Cliff, that fool son of mine, wants to put up a high-rise at the end of the boardwalk and most of the town is furious with him, now this—gossip—might be revealed. Neither should happen." Eleanor's eyes flashed with anger.

Her friend might be right, but she wasn't sure Eleanor would be able to stop either one from happening.

Eleanor sat on her porch long after Darlene left. Her fingers absently tapped the arm of her chair. The rhythm helped her think, to sort through the tangled knot of secrets and half-truths that had been woven around the Whitmore family name. The shadows crept across the lawn, but she hardly noticed the passage of time. Her mind was consumed with all Darlene had shared.

And, of course, there were also the letters

found in Jenna's house. Thank goodness Brent had no idea about them. The correspondence pointed to an affair between Vera and Lawrence, but it was all speculation, wasn't it? Events from a distant past, buried by time and fading memories.

But the possibility of an affair between Vera and Lawrence was all too real. It was all too much, too close to home. She'd long suspected something had happened between them, but suspicion was far different from proof.

Had Vera had an affair? Had she gone after what she wanted, even if it meant being cast aside by her family? Had she been foolish enough, strong enough, brave enough, to do it anyway?

A pain stabbed at her heart. She herself hadn't been that strong. Strong enough to choose what she wanted for her life instead of what her family had expected of her.

She shoved those thoughts far away. The problem now was Vera. Had her great-aunt thirsted for a life beyond the confines of their small island? Had her desires led her straight into the arms of a prince? And if so, what had become of their alleged affair?

She sighed heavily, her gaze fixed on a

bloom on the magnolia tree. It was all in the past, wasn't it? Just speculation and gossip from a bygone era. But even as she tried to convince herself of this, a nagging worry persisted. If word got out, if more people started digging...

No. She couldn't allow that to happen. The Whitmore name had to be protected, no matter the cost. She straightened in her chair, decision made. She would go to Brent herself and convince him to drop this line of inquiry, to leave the past where it belonged.

Rising slowly, she smoothed down her dress and gathered her resolve. She'd lived with secrets for so long. What was one more conversation to ensure they stayed buried?

"Winston, time for you to go inside. I have an errand to run." She let the dog slip inside and she turned around. As she made her way down the porch steps, she rehearsed her arguments in her head. It was all conjecture, after all. No self-respecting historian would publish something without concrete proof. And even if Brent had found some evidence, surely he could be made to see reason. The potential harm to living people, to families who had called Magnolia Key home for generations, surely that would give him pause.

He needed to understand the gravity of the situation and the possible consequences of his actions. She would make him see reason, one way or another.

Her steps quickened as she walked toward the Bayside Bed and Breakfast. She had to make Brent understand. The past was the past, and some things were better left undisturbed. As she approached the inn, she took a deep breath, steeling herself for the conversation ahead. She would do whatever it took to protect her family's legacy, to keep the secrets of the Whitmore family safely hidden away.

Brent sat on the porch of the Bayside Bed and Breakfast with his files spread out on the table beside him. The gentle breeze rustled the papers, and he absently placed a hand on them to keep them from flying away. He'd been poring over the documents for hours, trying to see if he could find any more information about Prince Lawrence.

As he reached for his glass of iced tea, a movement caught his eye. Miss Eleanor approached the B&B, her strides purposeful and her expression determined. He looked left and right, hoping to see Darlene and hoping Miss Eleanor was coming to see her, even though the woman looked straight at him.

"Mr. Dunn. I'd like a word with you." She climbed the stairs in front of him.

Nope, it was him. She was here to see him. He straightened in his chair, sensing this wasn't a casual visit.

He nodded, gesturing to the empty chair across from him. "Of course, Miss Eleanor. Please, have a seat."

Her eyes darted to the other end of the porch where an older couple sat chatting quietly. She lowered her voice as she settled into the chair. "We need to speak about what you found hidden in the wall here at the B&B."

His eyebrows rose in surprise. He hadn't expected her to broach the subject so directly. He leaned forward, matching her hushed tone. "You mean the letter to Vera?"

Her lips pressed into a thin line, and she gave a curt nod. "Yes, that letter. I understand you and Felicity have been quite… enthusiastic in your research about Prince Lawrence's time here on Magnolia Key."

He felt a mix of excitement and unease. On

the one hand, Eleanor might be about to provide some valuable information. On the other, her tone suggested she wasn't entirely pleased with their investigation.

"We've been trying to piece together the history," he explained carefully. "It's fascinating, really. The idea of having a sister island. The prince's frequent visits, the connections to the island…"

"Mr. Dunn," she interrupted, her voice sharp but still quiet. "I'm not here to encourage your curiosity. Quite the opposite, in fact."

Any chance of learning something more from Miss Eleanor deflated like a spent balloon, replaced by growing disappointment. "I'm not sure I understand, ma'am."

Her gaze scanned the porch once more before settling back on him. "I know you believe the letter that suggests she had a… ah… relationship with Prince Lawrence."

Brent nodded, his eyes meeting hers. "It did suggest they were quite close."

She tapped her finger on the table. "I'm here to ask you to stop digging into this matter." Her voice was firm, her gaze unwavering. "It's a private family issue, and I won't have any scandal attached to our name."

Brent leaned back in his chair, considering her words. "I understand your concern, Miss Eleanor. But as a historian, I have a responsibility to uncover the truth about the past, especially when it involves such a significant figure as Prince Lawrence."

"But the past is the past for a reason, Mr. Dunn. Some stories are better left untold, some secrets better kept."

Brent frowned, his researcher's instincts bristling at the idea of leaving any stone unturned. "But surely the truth is important? This could be a significant part of Magnolia Key's history. An *interesting* part."

"It's more than just history," she said, her voice taking on a hint of steel. "It's about real people, real lives. There are people who are still here, still affected by what happened all those years ago."

He sat back in his chair, studying her face. He could see the tension in her features, the way her hands gripped the arms of her chair. This wasn't just about protecting an old secret. There was something more personal at stake for her.

"Miss Eleanor," he began carefully, "I understand your concern. But I'm not looking to cause any trouble or pain. I'm just trying to understand the past, including my own family's connection to this island."

"But Mr. Dunn, sometimes the past is best left where it is. Not every story needs to be told, not every question needs an answer."

He sighed, torn between his desire to uncover the full story and his respect for Miss Eleanor's wishes. "I don't want to cause any distress for you or your family. But I also believe that history has a way of revealing itself, whether we like it or not."

She stood abruptly, her forehead creased with disapproval. "I hope you'll reconsider your stance, Mr. Dunn. For the sake of everyone involved." With that, she turned and walked away, leaving him alone with his thoughts.

He leaned back in his chair and stared out at the bay. What kind of researcher was he if he just let himself be persuaded to drop a story like this? One that involved a significant historical figure? And if he dropped it from his research and didn't publish it, what would prevent someone from coming along after him and uncovering the truth? It would look like he hadn't done a thorough job with his research.

Uneasiness settled over him. It seemed like he had an impossible decision to make.

There was no sign of Brent at breakfast the next morning. Felicity didn't know if that was good or bad. She'd thought he'd come and track her down to see if she'd told Gran about the letter. She brought in the last tray of dishes from the dining room. "Everyone's finished, Gran. You got quite a lot of compliments on the quiche this morning."

"I'm glad the guests enjoyed it. I haven't decided what we're having tomorrow. Need to make up my mind and get started on the prep."

She set the dishes by the dishwasher and started rinsing them. "I can help if you like. Or I can continue out in the shed. I've got about half of it sorted out. You'll be surprised about how much more storage you'll have."

Gran paused as she was putting a carton of cream in the fridge. "I still feel bad that you're tackling that project all on your own."

"It keeps me busy. And it's kind of fun going through all those boxes and seeing what's accumulated. I did find a box of board games. I thought I'd bring a few in and put them in the sitting room for the guests to use on rainy days."

"That's a good idea. I can't believe I let the shed get so out of control. It was an easy place to stash things and then stash more things. I kept meaning to organize it."

"Well, I'll soon have it organized for you and all the boxes labeled." She slipped the last dish in the dishwasher and turned it on. "I guess I'll head on out if we're finished here."

Gran reached out and stopped her. "First, I need you to know something. I went and talked to Eleanor yesterday. She would appreciate it if you and Brent stopped digging into Vera and Lawrence. It's in the past, anyway. You know Eleanor, she can't stand to think about people gossiping about her family."

"I understand. I'll talk to Brent. I don't want to upset Miss Eleanor or put a strain on your friendship."

"Thank you, dear. I appreciate it."

She headed outside, crossed the sunlit lawn, and opened the shed. She stepped inside, eyeing the stacks of boxes. There was still so much more to sort through. She got to work, continuing with her system of keep, pitch, or donate.

Sometime later, she was startled when she heard a noise at the door. She looked up to see Brent standing there, framed in light. Her heart fluttered quickly, though she ignored it. Friends, remember?

"Brent, hi."

"Darlene said you were out here." He stepped inside.

She stood and stretched. "Just working my way through all of this."

"I was wondering if you had a chance to show the letter to Darlene."

"I… I did. And she went to talked to Eleanor."

"I had a visit from Miss Eleanor myself."

"Gran thinks we should let the whole Prince Lawrence and Vera thing fade back away."

"Miss Eleanor was a bit more forceful than that with her request, but yes, I clearly got her message."

"So you'll just let it all drop?"

"I… I'm not sure. If I can find out this much, so can the next person researching the area."

"Maybe. Maybe not."

"A researcher normally doesn't hide from the truth." He frowned.

She put her hands on her hips. "Even if he's been asked not to stir up gossip? I mean, we don't know anything for certain."

"Don't we?" He raised an eyebrow. "Lawrence professed his love and was asking her to go away with him."

"But Vera never got the letter, did she? We don't know how it ended. Can't you just drop it?"

"I… I can't. Not until I know the truth. And then… then I'm not sure what I'll do."

"Why would you go against Miss Eleanor's wishes?"

"Because this might be a significant piece of the area's history. And I'll, of course, write about the sister island. A lot of the details will be out there. People might start remembering things. Talk. Gossip. And There's the pendant that Tori has. Dale knows it's the same one that was presumably lost when the prince visited. But Vera had it."

"I wish we never started looking into all of this."

"But we did. And now I have to see where it leads me."

"I think you should drop it." She waited for his reaction, waited to see if he'd do what she—and Miss Eleanor—asked him to do.

He looked at her for a long moment. "Duly noted." He turned and walked out of the shed.

Exasperation swept through her. He didn't understand what gossip like this could do to a family in a small town. He was all about his research. That meant more to him than how Miss Eleanor felt... or how she felt.

It was probably for the best that she hadn't let anything happen with Brent. She couldn't be a part of this any longer. Not if it upset Miss Eleanor this much. Not if Gran asked her to drop it. Even if she was still curious...

Or was she using all this to justify her decision to back off things with Brent?

Brent understood where Felicity was coming from. He did. Just like he understood Miss Eleanor's feelings. But he was a researcher at heart. How could he just let something like this drop out of his findings? He'd feel like a fraud writing about the history of the area and leaving out something as significant as Prince Lawrence's visits.

But he'd seen the anger and disappointment in both Miss Eleanor's and Felicity's eyes when he wouldn't bend to their demands.

He could leave out any mention of Vera though, couldn't he? But what if the next person coming along found out about her? Maybe he could write about Lawrence and Vera in a… gentler way.

He scowled, pushing aside any decision, and snapped open his laptop. Time to look into his own family and set the Whitmores aside for a bit. He searched online but found not many records were online for the area. In frustration, he closed his laptop, shoved it in his computer bag, and decided to head to the mainland to do some research in person.

He took the ferry, feeling its motors thrumming beneath him as it churned to a stop at the landing. He pulled his car off and made his way to his first stop at the county courthouse. He parked and got out of the car, his bag heavy with his laptop and handwritten notes.

Squinting against the bright sun, he glanced up at the building, a stately brick structure with imposing columns lining the front of it. He climbed the stairs and pushed through the heavy wooden doors. The blast of air conditioning was a welcome break from the Florida heat.

His footsteps echoed on the marble floor as he approached the clerk's desk, explaining his mission to search old records. The clerk, a friendly middle-aged woman with graying hair and laugh lines around her eyes, led him to a room filled with dusty tomes and microfiche readers. "Good luck," she said with a smile. "The Wi-Fi password is history." She smiled. "I know, not very secure, right? Let me know if you need any help. Oh, and don't forget to take some breaks. It's easy to lose track of time here." With a knowing wink, she turned and left him alone with his task.

He stood for a moment, absorbing the quiet energy of the room. The history just waiting to be discovered. He set his bag down and got to work.

He spent hours poring over the records, his eyes straining in the dim light. Finally, he found what he was looking for—deed records and a census listing the Burton family. He smiled at his success as he printed off copies. He scribbled down the information in his notes, feeling a connection to his past growing stronger with each discovery.

Next, he drove to the local historical society, housed in a quaint Victorian-era home. The volunteer at the front desk seemed thrilled to have a visitor interested in local history. She eagerly showed him to their archives.

In a quiet corner of the building, he carefully leafed through yellowed documents and faded photographs. His persistence paid off when he stumbled upon his mother's baptism records. "Joan Burton," he whispered, tracing his finger over the name. Daughter of William and Mary Burton.

As the afternoon wore on, Brent's excitement grew with each new piece of information he uncovered. He felt like a detective, piecing together the puzzle of his family's past.

Just as he was about to call it a day, a small newspaper clipping caught his eye. It was an obituary for his grandmother. Brent's heart skipped as he read the details, but then he froze. Something wasn't right.

The obituary stated that his grandmother

was survived by a daughter and a son. Brent frowned, his brow creasing in confusion. The date of her death was after the hurricane that had supposedly claimed Jonah's life.

He read the article again, trying to make sense of this new information. How could his uncle have survived his grandmother if he'd died in the hurricane? Had Miss Eleanor been mistaken? Or was there more to this story than he'd been told?

He couldn't wait to get back to the island and share the news with Felicity. See if she had any ideas about the discrepancy regarding Jonah. But then he remembered. She'd ask him to quit digging into the island's history. She wouldn't be pleased with yet another mystery.

He gathered his things and headed out to his car. Time to go home. Well, not home. Back to Magnolia Key. Even though it had started to feel like home to him, it wasn't, he reminded himself. It was just somewhere he was staying while he did his research.

He parked his car on the ferry and went up top, leaning against the railing, his eyes fixed on the horizon as the sun dipped lower, painting the sky in vibrant purples and streaks of orange. The gentle rumble of the engine and the lapping of waves against the hull filled the air, but he barely noticed. His mind was a whirlwind of thoughts and emotions.

He couldn't help but think back to that evening not so long ago when he and Felicity had shared this same view. They had stood side by side, their hands brushing, a thread of connection and possibility between them. Now, he stood alone, the space beside him feeling oddly empty.

The cool sea breeze tousled his hair, and he closed his eyes for a moment, trying to make sense of how quickly things had changed. He and Felicity had been so in sync, working together to unravel the mysteries of Magnolia Key. Now, it felt like an invisible wall had sprung up between them.

His hand unconsciously tightened on the railing. He understood Felicity's hesitation, her desire to respect Miss Eleanor's wishes. But the researcher in him couldn't let go of the tantalizing threads of history he'd uncovered. The prince's visits, the hidden letter, and now the puzzling discrepancy about his uncle Jonah's fate—it all swirled in his mind, pieces of a puzzle he was desperate to solve.

He opened his eyes. The first stars began to

appear as the sky darkened into a slate gray. The island grew larger as they approached. He sighed, running a hand through his hair. How had they gone from that moment of near intimacy to barely speaking? The mass of unspoken words and unresolved feelings hung between them like a heavy fog.

As the ferry chugged steadily toward the island, he found himself at a crossroads. Should he pursue the truth, potentially alienating Felicity and the islanders further? Or should he let it go, leaving the mysteries of Magnolia Key —and his own family history—buried in the past?

The last rays of sunlight disappeared below the horizon, and he turned away from the railing. With heavy footsteps he made his way to his car. Hard decisions had to be made.

As the ferry approached the island dock, he couldn't shake the feeling that although he was nearing the island, a chasm of distance remained between him and Felicity. And maybe a chasm between him and the whole town of Magnolia Key.

CHAPTER 19

Felicity barely saw Brent the next few days. He'd pop in for breakfast but didn't really chat with her. Just a simple good morning. He didn't bring his research down with him like he used to. He just ate his breakfast quickly and disappeared.

"Felicity, why don't you get out today? Take a break? You've been helping me and cleaning out that shed. You need a break." Gran took the last of the dishes from her hands.

"But I haven't finished with the shed."

"It will keep. Why don't you do a little shopping in town? Go out for lunch. It's better than moping around here." Gran looked at her pointedly.

"I'm not moping…"

Gran just raised an eyebrow, not bothering to reply.

She let out a long sigh. "Okay, maybe I am." *Wasn't Gran always right?* "I'll go into town for a bit if you're sure you don't need me."

"Go. Shoo. Have a good time. The fresh air will do you good too."

She headed outside, away from the B&B, and away from the possibility of running into Brent.

She strolled along the sun-dappled sidewalks of Magnolia Key's main street, her sandals slapping against the pavement. The quaint storefronts beckoned with their colorful displays, but she found herself merely window shopping, her mind elsewhere.

She drifted into Seaside Treasures, running her fingers over delicate seashell necklaces and inhaling the aroma of coconut-scented candles. She lingered in front of a display of magazines, then picked up a romance novel with a sunset-kissed couple on the cover. With a sigh, she set it back down. The shopkeeper smiled warmly, but Felicity just nodded and slipped back out onto the street.

As the afternoon wore on, her stomach

growled. She realized she'd skipped breakfast in her haste to avoid another awkward encounter with Brent. The familiar awning of Coastal Coffee came into view, and she quickened her pace.

As she pushed open the door, the aroma of freshly brewed coffee and warm pastries welcomed her, instantly soothing her frazzled nerves.

"Felicity!" Beverly's warm voice called out. Before she could respond, she found herself wrapped in a hug. "It's so good to see you, honey."

"Hey, Beverly," she said, returning the embrace. "It's good to see you too."

Beverly held her at arm's length, studying her face. "You look like you could use a good meal and some company. The lunch rush is dying down. Mind if I join you?"

She felt a genuine smile spread across her face for the first time that day. "That would be wonderful."

She settled into a cozy booth, grateful for the familiar comfort of the cafe. Beverly returned and set down two steaming bowls of soup and a plate of assorted tiny sandwiches.

"So, I could tell something was wrong as

soon as you walked in. Care to talk about it?" Beverly reached for a small triangle sandwich.

"I don't know what to do," she admitted, reaching for her glass of iced tea. "I used to love teaching so much. It was my whole world. But now…" she trailed off, staring into the dark liquid.

Beverly reached across the table to give Felicity's hand a gentle squeeze. "What changed, honey?"

She sighed. "Everything and nothing. The kids are still great, but there's so much pressure now. Test scores, angry parents, budget cuts. And then there's all the safety drills…" She shuddered slightly. "I used to feel like I was making a difference, you know? Now I just feel drained."

"That sounds tough," Beverly said softly. "Have you thought about what else you might want to do?"

She shook her head. "That's just it. I've been a teacher for so long, I don't know who I am without it. What else could I even do?"

Beverly took a sip of her tea, considering. "You know, sometimes we get so caught up in what we think we should be doing, we forget to listen to what our heart is telling us."

"But how do I figure that out?" she asked, frustration creeping into her voice.

"Well, what makes you happy? What are you passionate about?" Beverly's eyes twinkled. "Besides that handsome historian staying at your Gran's place, of course."

Her cheeks flushed. And anyway, there wasn't anything between her and Brent anymore. He was totally avoiding her. "Ah, Brent and I… we're having a bit of a disagreement these days."

"Something you can work out?"

"I'm not certain."

"That's probably adding to the stress of your decision, isn't it?" Beverly paused, looking thoughtful. "But seriously, think about what lights you up. What makes you lose track of time?"

She nibbled on a sandwich, pondering. "I do love history. And I've really enjoyed helping Brent with his research. It's been exciting, uncovering all these stories about the island." She shrugged. "Well, back when I was helping him."

Beverly nodded encouragingly. "That's a start. Maybe There's a way to combine your love of teaching with your passion for history.

You don't have to figure it all out right away, you know. Sometimes we need to give ourselves permission to explore and try new things."

"I guess I'm just scared," she admitted. "What if I make the wrong choice?"

"Oh, honey," Beverly said, her voice warm with understanding. "There's no such thing as a wrong choice, not really. Every decision we make teaches us something. The only real mistake is not listening to your heart and not giving yourself a chance to grow."

She felt a tiny bit of the weight she'd been carrying around lift from her shoulders. "I guess I've been so focused on what I might be losing, I haven't thought about what I might gain."

"That's the spirit." Beverly smiled. "And remember, you've got a whole island full of people who love you and want to see you happy. You're not alone in this, hon."

"Thanks, Beverly."

"And it wouldn't hurt to try and work things out with Brent, either." She gave one more piece of advice before turning back to their meal.

They ate their lunch and their conversation turned to the weather, some new books that had been donated to the lending library here at the cafe, and a predicted cool front. Just simple, everyday conversation. And so welcome. And so… ordinary. She craved more days just like these.

As they finished their meal, she felt a glimmer of hope. She might not have all the answers yet, but she felt excited about the possibilities ahead.

And she knew the first thing she needed to do. Let the school know she wasn't returning.

Felicity practically skipped back to the B&B, beaming the entire time. She couldn't wait to talk to Gran. She flung open the door and burst into the kitchen. "Gran? You here?"

"Right here." Gran emerged from the pantry, wiping her hands on her apron. "Oh, before I forget, There's a letter for you on the counter."

She went to the counter, her smile fading as she recognized the school district's logo. She tore open the envelope, scanned its contents, and set it down with a small exhale.

"Who's it from?"

"The school district. They've lost some funding and they're making more budget cuts."

"Oh, that's too bad. That's terrible news." Gran's face creased with concern.

A smile tugged at the corners of her mouth and she saw the surprise in Gran's eyes when it turned into a grin. "Actually, it's perfect timing. They need to let teachers go, and… I'm going to be one of them."

"They fired you?" Gran's eyes widened.

"No, no. But I had a heart-to-heart talk with Beverly. She's really wise, you know?" She grinned again. "And I made a decision. I'm not going back to teach this year. I'll call them to tell them. I'm thinking they'll be glad to have one less teacher to let go. And I believe this letter is a sign that I've made the right choice."

Gran hugged her. "I'm so happy you've made a decision. I know it's been weighing on you since you got here."

"It's been weighing on me for a few years now." She frowned. "Of course, I don't know what I'm going to do with my life now."

"You're going to stay right here—if you want to. You can work here at the B&B until you decide what you might want to do. I love having you here."

"You sure, Gran?"

"Oh, I'm so sure. I can't think of anything

I'd love more." Gran reached out and touched her cheek. "You bring such joy to my life, Felicity. I still remember the very first time I held you in my arms. It was like nothing I've ever experienced. And my love for you has only grown stronger over the years."

Tears sprang to her eyes, and she cupped her hand over Gran's. "I love you too, Gran. So much."

Gran cleared her throat. "Okay, now that all of that's settled. I've got some bread to bake."

"Oh, can I knead the dough?"

Gran chuckled. "Some things never change. It always was your favorite part of bread baking."

"Why aren't you getting ready?" Gran frowned at Felicity when she saw her in shorts and a tee shirt.

"Ready for what?" Though she knew exactly what Gran was talking about.

"You're going to Brent's talk, aren't you? Going to support him?"

She let out a long sigh. "I'm sure he'd rather I not go. He's done a great job of avoiding me. Things are just so awkward between us now. And he wouldn't listen to me when I asked him to drop the whole Vera and Lawrence thing."

"Do you think he'll bring that up at his talk?" Gran's forehead creased in concern.

"I honestly have no idea."

Gran shook her head. "I guess we'll see."

She gave her a no-nonsense look. "Now go upstairs and change. Five minutes. Then we're leaving."

She knew there was no use in arguing with Gran. She hurried upstairs to slip into something nicer than shorts and the stained tee shirt she'd been wearing to clean out the shed.

They walked into the community center about five minutes before Brent's scheduled talk. Beverly sat over by the wall with her friend, Maxine, and waved to her.

"There's Eleanor. Let's go sit by her." Gran pointed to some empty chairs.

She settled into her seat next to Gran, acutely aware of Miss Eleanor's rigid posture beside them. The older woman's face remained impassive, giving no hint of her thoughts or feelings about the upcoming presentation.

"Good evening, Miss Eleanor," she said, hoping to break the tension.

Miss Eleanor simply nodded, her eyes fixed on the stage. "Hello."

She shot Gran a quick look, and Gran just shrugged slightly. Her stomach churned with anxiety as she watched Brent approach the podium. He looked confident in his pressed shirt and slacks, but she could see the slight tremor in his hands as he arranged his notes. The buzz of conversation in the room slowly died down as people took their seats and turned their attention to the front.

As Brent cleared his throat to begin, she found herself rubbing her palms along her thighs. What would he say? Had he decided to include the information about Prince Lawrence and Vera, despite her asking him not to? Despite Miss Eleanor's pleas? She glanced sideways at Miss Eleanor, wondering how the proud woman would react if Brent revealed her family's long-buried secrets.

The room fell silent, all eyes on Brent. She held her breath, her heart pounding as she waited for him to speak. Whatever he said in the next few moments could change everything—for Miss Eleanor and for Felicity's own sense of belonging on Magnolia Key, since so many people knew she'd been helping Brent with his research.

She sat unmoving in her chair as Brent began his presentation. His voice was steady and professional, but she could detect a hint of nervousness in the way he gripped the edges of the podium.

"Good afternoon, everyone. Thank you for

coming out today," Brent said, his eyes scanning the room. "I've been researching the southwest Gulf Coast area of Florida for a book I'm hoping to publish."

She held her breath, her heart racing as she waited to see if he would mention Vera and Lawrence. She glanced at Miss Eleanor, whose face remained an impassive mask.

"I've discovered a wealth of information about this area's rich history," he continued. "In fact, I've even uncovered a personal connection to the region that I never knew existed."

Her muscles tensed. Would he reveal the secret? But as Brent dove into the details of early settlements and the development of the coastal communities, she gradually began to relax. He spoke about the fishing industry, the impact of hurricanes, and the evolution of tourism, but not once did he mention Prince Lawrence or Vera.

Relief washed over her. She took another quick look at Miss Eleanor and saw the slightest easing of the older woman's shoulders. Gran caught her eye and gave a small, approving nod.

As he wrapped up his presentation, she felt a mix of emotions. Pride in Brent's professionalism, gratitude for his discretion, and a lingering sadness about the distance that had grown between them.

"Thank you all for your attention," Brent said. "I'd be happy to answer any questions you might have."

Several hands shot up, and Brent called on a man in the back row. "You mentioned researching the area's history. Have you found out anything about the sister island relationship Magnolia Key had back in the 1920s? An island called Bardonzia?"

Her breath caught in her throat. She saw Brent hesitate for just a moment, his eyes flicking briefly in her direction before he answered.

"I have done some research into that. It is rather fascinating that the islands around here had sister islands—such close relationships with foreign countries."

She didn't dare move a muscle.

"But I haven't finished with my research into that area yet."

She let out a small breath.

"Any more questions?" He asked.

He answered a few more questions from the crowd, but none of them veered toward the prince and Vera. He ended his presentation to a smattering of applause.

Miss Eleanor rose from her seat, looked at Gran and her, and just nodded before walking away without a word.

Gran leaned close. "I'm glad he did the right thing."

She nodded. But that didn't mean he wouldn't write about it and put it in his book. But for now, at least, Miss Eleanor's family had been spared.

Brent stood at the window in his room, watching the evening slip in over the water. The stars blinked up above in a sight that still amazed him with their clarity. Moonlight spilled across the tops of the waves as they rolled endlessly to shore.

He thought his presentation had gone well today. And he'd successfully dodged the question about Bardonzia. He hadn't missed the looks that Miss Eleanor had sent in his direction when he'd first come out on the stage, then her face had remained impassive the rest of his talk.

He frankly had been surprised to see Felicity

in the crowd. Then, once he'd known she was there, he'd hoped that she and Darlene would come up to talk to him after his presentation. But as the crowd faded away, both of them were gone.

He didn't know who was avoiding whom more. He or Felicity. He wanted to talk to her, but he couldn't give her the one thing she wanted. An assurance that nothing would be said about Vera and Lawrence.

He turned back to the desk and opened his laptop. Now that his presentation was over, he wanted to devote more time to his own family's history. The laptop cast a low glow over the table as his fingers flew over the keys, researching anything he could find on a Jonah Burton.

He rubbed his eyes and leaned closer to his laptop screen, his eyes scanning through the search results for "Jonah Burton." He'd been at this for hours, methodically sifting through information, eliminating possibilities one by one.

A Jonah Burton who'd been a schoolteacher in Georgia? No, that probably wasn't him. Another who'd worked as a farmhand in Alabama? Possibly, but unlikely. Brent clicked through page after page, his determination growing with each dead end. But then, maybe his grandmother's obituary was wrong and Jonah had died in the hurricane. He began to lose hope.

Then something caught his eye. A Jonah Burton who had worked at the port in Port Everglades. His pulse quickened. This could be it. He remembered that his uncle had worked at the marina here on Magnolia Key. It made sense that he might have found similar work elsewhere.

He pulled up a map on his screen, his fingers tapping impatiently as he waited for it to load. When it did, he let out a low whistle. Port Everglades was on the other side of the state, but it was only two and a half hours away.

He zoomed in on the route, noticing a stretch of road that cut straight across the state. "Alligator Alley," he murmured, recalling hearing locals mention it before. It was a direct shot from one coast to the other through the Everglades.

He sat back in his chair and rubbed his chin. He could make that drive easily. He could go there and see what he could find out in person. Records, people who might have known Jonah —maybe someone had known him.

He glanced at his watch. It was late, but his mind was scrambling with possibilities. He could leave first thing in the morning and be there before lunch. The prospect of uncovering more about his family's history, about the possibility of an uncle he'd never known, was too tempting to ignore.

He began to plan. He'd let Darlene know he'd be gone for the day. He'd have to gather some documents, just in case. But mostly, he needed to be prepared for whatever he might discover.

CHAPTER 21

The next morning, Felicity woke up at the first light. She hurried to get up so she could help Gran with breakfast. She hummed under her breath as she slipped on her clothes, realizing how much lighter she felt since she'd made her decision to quit her teaching position. The school had gratefully accepted her resignation, and the principal had said he was sorry to see her go. Now, she just had to figure out what to do with her life from now on. But working here with Gran was a good middle ground.

She went down the back stairs into the kitchen because it was quicker—not to avoid Brent, of course. Gran was busy frying bacon.

She went over and kissed her on the cheek. "Morning."

"Morning. Did you sleep well?"

"I did."

Gran eyed her. "And Brent left for the day, so you can quit trying to avoid him this morning."

She laughed. "I wasn't."

"Right." Gran smiled patiently as she turned back to the skillet.

"Where did he go? Did he say?" She kept her voice nonchalant, as if she were just making conversation, not like she really cared.

Gran glanced back over her shoulder. "He didn't say, just that he'd be gone most of the day."

She was kind of sorry she'd missed him. She did wonder if he'd found anything else about his family and had tentatively—*possibly*—planned on asking him today. She couldn't avoid him forever, could she?

As if Gran could read her thoughts, she turned from the stove, spatula in hand. "Now that you've made your decision, don't you think it's time to talk to Brent? Wasn't the uncertainty about your decision regarding teaching part of the reason you were leery about starting up a relationship with him? But that's been decided now."

"I still don't know what I'm going to do if I'm not a teacher."

"But you have a place to live and time to figure that out. And you seem… happier now that you're not returning to your teaching job."

"I have to admit that I do feel a sense of relief. A great sense of relief." She grabbed a stack of plates from the cabinet, hoping to distract Gran from this line of questioning.

"So why don't you talk to him?"

Well, that didn't work.

She let out a sigh. "We're still in disagreement on the whole Lawrence and Vera thing. I asked him not to print anything about it. He said he couldn't promise me that."

"You know he's only doing what he thinks is right as a researcher. For his professional reputation. As much as I hope the story about Vera and the prince remains buried, I do understand where Brent is coming from."

"I guess I can see his side," she admitted reluctantly. "But Miss Eleanor will be very upset if all this comes out."

Gran nodded. "She will. But gossip always dies down eventually. And she can't undo the past. Vera made choices. And there are always consequences of our choices."

Consequences of our choices.

Like when she'd pushed Brent away. Told him they should just be friends. And now? They were even less than friends.

A consequence of her choice.

Brent navigated his car onto the long stretch of highway known as Alligator Alley. The early morning sun cast a warm light over the flat landscape, illuminating the vast expanse of the Everglades that surrounded him on either side of the road, an endless sea of sawgrass marshes and cypress swamps. He turned on the radio, letting the music fill the car as his thoughts drifted to the purpose of his trip—hopefully uncovering more information about his uncle, Jonah Burton.

As he drove, anticipation and uncertainty churned through him. The obituary he'd found for his grandmother contradicted what he'd been told about his uncle's fate. This discrepancy had sparked a burning curiosity within him, a need to uncover the truth about his family's past.

The miles ticked by, and Brent found himself wondering what he might discover in Port Everglades. Was the Jonah Burton who had worked at the port truly his uncle? If so, why had everyone on Magnolia Key thought he died in the hurricane? The questions swirled in his mind, each one fueling his desire to find answers.

He passed an alligator basking on the banks of the canals that ran alongside the highway. Then in a few miles, he passed another. It appeared the roadway was appropriately named.

The sun began to rise higher in the sky as he continued his drive, the endless stretches of swampland giving way to signs of civilization as he neared the coast.

As the skyline of Fort Lauderdale came into view, his pulse quickened. He reminded himself that this might be a wild goose chase. He might find out nothing. But still, he had hope. He exited the highway and made his way toward the port area.

As he pulled into a parking lot near the port, he took a deep breath to steady himself. He sat in the car for a moment, gathering his thoughts and mentally preparing for whatever he might discover.

A large cruise ship rose up in the distance as a steady line of cars crept toward the parking garage. He crossed over and spoke to a security person, explaining his mission. The man gave him directions to the nearby administration building and suggested he ask his questions there.

At the administration building, he entered the lobby and crossed over to the desk where yet another security person worked.

"Good morning. I have kind of a strange request. I'm looking for my… my uncle."

"His name?" The man sat with his hands poised over a computer.

"Well, I'm not sure he even worked here. Or if the Jonah Burton I saw referenced as working here at one time is the same Jonah Burton I'm looking for."

The man typed into his computer. "We have a Jonah Burton working here now."

Shock skittered through him. Could it be this easy? "You do? Now?"

"Shall I call him? He'd have to come down here to meet with you."

"Ah, yes. Could you do that?"

"Sure. Just take a seat over there." The man motioned to a bank of chairs across the lobby.

He walked over and sat down. Then got back up and paced a few times before going to stand by the windows looking out over a vast yard with boats hoisted up on platforms and being worked on. He turned at the sound of footsteps approaching.

He stared at the man coming closer, his pulse thudding as he noticed a striking resemblance to his mother. The same warm brown eyes, the same slight tilt of the head as he walked. The man was older, with gray streaks in his hair and lines etched around his eyes, but there was no mistaking the family resemblance.

The man stopped a few feet away, studying him with a creased brow. Brent could see the confusion and curiosity in his expression, mirroring his own emotions.

Taking in a long, slow breath, he asked, "Are you Jonah Burton?"

The man nodded slowly. "I am. Do I know you?"

His throat felt dry as he struggled to find the right words. "My name is Brent Dunn. My mother was Joan Burton. I think… I think you might be my uncle."

Jonah's eyebrows shot up, and he took a step closer, scrutinizing Brent's face. "You're Joanie's boy? I didn't even know she had a son."

He nodded, a lump forming in his throat at the mention of his mother's name. "Yes, that's right. Joan was my mother."

Jonah's expression softened, a mix of emotions flickering across his face. "I can't believe it. You look so much like her." He paused, staring hard, as if drinking in every detail. "Joanie had a boy. How could I not know that?"

"I'm not sure. Mom died when I was a young boy. My father's family never told me anything about my mom's family."

"But how did you find me? I thought… well, it's been so long."

"It's a long story," he said, feeling overwhelmed by the sudden connection. "I've been researching my family history, and I came across some information that led me here. I honestly wasn't sure if I'd find anything."

"And yet you did." The man never took his eyes off him.

"I've been researching the history of

Southwest Florida. I'm staying on Magnolia Key."

Jonah's eyes lit up with recognition.

"And what I found out in Magnolia Key is that…" He paused, staring at Jonah. "That you died in a hurricane."

Jonah slowly nodded. "I heard that rumor."

"And you did nothing to correct it?"

Jonah glanced around the lobby, then back at him. "This isn't really the place for a reunion like this. How long are you in town? Maybe we could grab a coffee or something?"

He nodded eagerly. "I'd like that. I have so many questions if you're willing to answer them."

A shadow passed over Jonah's face, but he managed a small smile. "I'm sure you do. And I'll do my best to answer what I can. How about we meet at the diner down the street in about an hour? I need to wrap up a few things here first."

"That sounds perfect," he agreed, eager for more details. He'd come looking for answers, and now he was face-to-face with a living piece of his family's history. He had an uncle. Family.

As Jonah turned to leave, he called out, "Uncle Jonah?" The word felt strange on his tongue, but right somehow.

Jonah paused, looking back at him with a questioning gaze.

"Thank you," he said simply. "For agreeing to meet with me."

Jonah's expression softened again, and he nodded. "Of course. We're family, after all." With that, he headed back into the depths of the building, leaving Brent standing in the lobby, his mind reeling from the unexpected encounter.

Brent sat at the diner, checking his watch. It had been over an hour and no sign of Jonah. What if he didn't show up? He had disappeared from everyone's lives before. Was he doing it again? The minutes ticked by slowly.

He finally looked up and saw Jonah hurrying inside. Jonah slipped into the seat across from him. "Sorry, I'm late. Took me longer than I thought to wrap things up."

"No problem." He was just glad Jonah showed up.

They both ordered burgers, fries, and malts. Jonah took his long-handled spoon and stirred his malt. "So, I guess you have questions?"

"I do. Like why does everyone on Magnolia Key think you're dead?"

"The day of the hurricane, I was out by the marina. I was supposed to… to meet someone. They never showed up. So I started helping secure the boats when the hurricane hit. I was swept out into the bay. The other workers saw it happen."

"But you didn't die. Obviously."

"No, I caught hold of part of a boat floating by and eventually washed up on shore down the coast. I was pretty banged up and someone took me to the hospital. When I was discharged about a week later, I made my way back to my parents' house." He smiled slightly. "Joanie threw herself into my arms when I walked in the door, and Mom broke into tears."

"But… why does everyone think you died?"

"It's… complicated. I thought it best that I just disappear. If everyone thought I was dead, so much the better."

"Were you in some kind of trouble?" He frowned, not following all his uncle's words.

"I…" Jonah's forehead crinkled. "Let's say it was a matter of the heart. And if people found out I was alive, and found out about it—well, about my little matter—it could complicate my parents' lives too. So we all decided to move away. My parents moved to Miami with Joanie. I ended up going overseas. Working in different ports in Europe."

"Didn't you come back and visit?"

"Only once. Before Joanie married. I got sporadic letters from home. It usually took the letters quite a while to catch up with me. And phone calls were way out of our budgets, not that I really had a phone in most places I stayed." Jonah looked up as sadness clouded his eyes. "I got a letter from Dad telling me Mom died. I got home as soon as I could, but it had been almost a year since he sent the letter. Dad was gone by then too. New people lived in their house, and all my parents' things were gone. Their neighbor told me that Joanie had died too. The shock of that crushed me. And I think the loss of both of them was too much for Dad. I should have been there for him."

"I'm sorry. That must have been very hard."

"It was. I went back to Europe to work because I couldn't bear being home. But eventually, I moved back to the States. Got a job here at the port. Been here for years."

"And you never went back to Magnolia Key?"

"Not once. There's no reason to. Any reason for me to return was taken away from me."

He started to put the pieces together. "So you were in love with someone on the island? Was that it?"

Jonah nodded with a hint of reluctance. "I was. But she was to marry someone else. She chose him over me. It broke my heart, but I understood. I had nothing to give her… but my love. Ellie came from money. And she never would have gone against her family's wishes."

He frowned. "Ellie?" No, it couldn't be? Could it?

"Yes, my Ellie. Eleanor Whitmore. Though I supposed she's Eleanor Griffin now since she married Theodore Griffin."

He sat back in his seat, his mouth dropping open. "You and Miss Eleanor?"

Jonah's lips curved in a small smile. "I know. An unlikely match. But we fell in love. But Eleanor was supposed to marry Theodore, a much more suitable match. So when everyone thought I was drowned in the storm, well, it made sense to just let them keep believing that, and to disappear. It made her choice easier."

Jonah and Miss Eleanor. He could barely wrap his mind around the thought.

"So you know Ellie?"

"I… do. She's, ah, not pleased with me right now, but that's another story for another time."

"How is she?"

"She's fine, I guess. Lives alone with her dog, Winston."

"Alone? Where's Theodore?"

"I take it he's been gone for many years."

Jonah sat back in his seat. "Really?"

He leaned forward. "Yes. She's alone now." He paused, treading carefully. "Why don't you drive back with me to the island? Wouldn't you like to see it again? I'm staying at the Bayside B&B. It's a nice place. Right on the bay."

"The old boardinghouse?"

He smiled. "Yes, the very one."

Jonah rubbed his face, then looked out the window. "Go and visit the island again?"

"Yes, come with me. We can talk more. We'll get you a room at the B&B. Come stay for a bit. We can get to know each other. I still have so many questions."

Jonah nodded slowly. "I think that just might be a fine idea. Maybe it's time to face the past. I haven't seen the island since the day the hurricane hit."

CHAPTER 22

Felicity and Gran were in the sitting room knitting when the door opened and Brent walked in with another man. Felicity put her knitting down and walked over to them. "Brent, you're back," she stated the obvious.

"I am."

Gran crossed over to them and stared intently at the man for a moment. She reached out and grabbed Felicity's arm, steadying herself, and gasped as she continued to focus on the man's face. Finally, she said, "Jonah?"

"Darlene, good to see you," the man said quietly.

"But… I thought…"

Gran looked like she'd seen a ghost. Felicity

looked from Gran to the man, and back to Gran.

"The facts of my death were greatly exaggerated." He smiled softly.

"But why didn't you tell us?" Gran's forehead creased.

"It was better for people to think I was gone."

"You mean, Eleanor?"

The man's eyes widened. "You… knew?"

"I knew. But Eleanor didn't know I knew. She thought it was her secret." Gran frowned. "You know, it broke her heart when she heard you died."

"It was best for her. Made things easier." He shrugged. "And my family sure didn't want to tangle with the Whitmores. Mr. Whitmore would have made it impossible for my parents to find work if I crossed him. I couldn't do that to them. Besides, Theodore was a good match for Ellie."

Gran snorted. Felicity looked at her grandmother in surprise. "Gran?"

"Theodore was a horrible match for Eleanor. There was no love between them their whole marriage. She just went through the motions for so many years. When he died, I almost think she was relieved. She could just live her life on her own terms then."

"I… didn't know. I thought she'd be happy with him. They were… similar. Came from similar backgrounds."

"Theodore Griffin was a cold…"

Felicity was almost sure Gran was going to curse—*which she never did*—but caught herself.

Gran continued, "Ah… a cold man. He controlled everything about what Eleanor could say or do. It was disheartening to watch. But I do feel like she's found some peace now."

"I'm glad to hear that."

"I'm not understanding all of this," she finally said. "Gran? Brent?"

Brent turned to her. "Felicity, meet my uncle, Jonah Burton. Jonah, this is Felicity, Darlene's granddaughter. Darlene owns the B&B."

Jonah held out his hand. "Pleased to meet you."

She shook his hand as if it was completely normal to shake the hand of a dead man.

Brent turned to Gran. "Darlene, I was hoping you had a room for Jonah. He's going to stay for a few days."

"Of course. Yes. Jonah, please stay. Come,

and let me get you checked in." Gran turned to her. "Why don't you and Brent go sit out on the porch for a bit? I think you have some catching up to do."

Felicity led Brent out to the porch. They took seats side by side as she tried to process everything she'd heard. "So... Jonah is your uncle?"

"He is. I can't believe I have family. It's like a miracle."

"I'm happy for you, Brent. I am. But how did you find him?"

"I found an obituary for my mother. It said she had a living daughter and son. So I started doing some digging."

A pang went through her that she hadn't been at his side when he was researching. Wasn't with him when he went looking for clues about his uncle. Missed seeing them meet each other for the first time.

"I'm glad you found him. You're a good researcher."

"It sure came in handy this time."

She took a deep breath, her heart skipping a

beat as she turned to face Brent. "Can we talk about something else for a minute?"

His brow creased slightly, but he nodded. "Of course. What's on your mind?"

She clasped her hands together, trying to steady her nerves. "I've been doing a lot of thinking lately. About my life, my career, and what I really want." She paused, searching for the right words. "I've decided not to go back to teaching in the fall."

His eyes widened in surprise. "Wow, that's a big decision. What made you choose that?"

She shrugged, a small smile tugging at her lips. "A lot of things, I guess. Being here on Magnolia Key, helping Gran with the B&B, and working on this research project with you… It's made me realize that I want more than just the same routine I've been stuck in for years."

She looked out at the water, the gentle waves rippling through the bay. "I don't have everything figured out yet, but I know I want to explore new possibilities."

He reached out and took her hand, his touch warm and comforting. "I think that's great. You have so much potential, you have so many choices stretching out ahead of you. I know you'll find something that truly makes you happy."

Her heart swelled at his words, and she turned to face him fully. "There's something else I wanted to talk to you about, too."

He tilted his head, his brown eyes searching hers. "What is it?"

She took another deep breath, gathering her courage. "I was thinking… maybe we could give each other a chance? To see where this thing between us might go?"

His expression softened, a smile spreading across his features. "I'd like that, Felicity. I really would."

He reached up and brushed a strand of hair from her face, his touch sending a shiver through her. "I know we've had our ups and downs, with the research and everything that's happened. But I can't deny that I've grown to care for you deeply."

Her heart soared at his words, and she leaned into his touch. "I care for you too, Brent. More than I ever expected to."

They sat there for a moment, lost in each other's eyes, the sound of the night and the distant chatter from inside the B&B fading away. His hand cupped her cheek, and he leaned in closer, his breath warm against her skin.

Her eyes fluttered closed, and she tilted her head up to meet his lips, knowing he was going to kiss her.

She leaned in, anticipating the warmth of his lips on hers. But just as they were about to connect, the porch door swung open with a creak.

"Hey, Brent." Jonah's voice shattered the moment. "How about a nightcap? We've got a lot of catching up to do."

She pulled back abruptly, her cheeks flushing as she tried to compose herself. Brent cleared his throat, looking a bit flustered himself.

"Uh, sure. That sounds great," Brent said, rising from his seat. He glanced at her, an apologetic look in his eyes. "We'll continue our talk later?"

She nodded, offering a small smile. "Of course. Go on, you two have a lot to discuss."

As Brent followed Jonah inside, she let out a long breath, her fingers tracing her lips where Brent's had almost touched. She gazed out at the moonlit water, her mind reeling from everything that had happened.

A few minutes later, the porch door opened

again. This time, it was Gran who stepped out, a knowing smile on her face.

"Mind if I join you, sweetheart?" Gran asked, settling into the chair Brent had vacated.

"Of course not," she replied, grateful for her grandmother's company.

They sat in comfortable silence for a moment, listening to the sound of the breeze blowing through the trees. In the distance, the sound of the ferry's horn announced its arrival.

Finally, Gran spoke up. "So, you and Brent seemed to be having quite the conversation out here."

She felt her face grow warm again. "We were just talking about… well, everything that's happened. And maybe… about us."

Gran's eyes twinkled. "I see. And how do you feel about that?"

"Honestly? I'm not sure," she admitted. "It's all happening so fast. First, deciding to leave teaching, and now these feelings for Brent. It's a lot to process."

Gran reached over and patted Felicity's hand. "Change can be overwhelming, dear. But it can also be exactly what we need sometimes."

She nodded, mulling over her

grandmother's words. "I just hope I'm making the right decisions."

"There's no guarantee in life, Felicity," Gran said softly. "But following your heart? That's never the wrong choice."

They fell into another comfortable silence, the night air cool and salty around them. Her mind wandered to Brent and Jonah, imagining the stories they must be sharing inside.

"It's quite something, isn't it?" Gran mused as if reading her mind. "Jonah coming back after all these years. Life has a way of surprising us when we least expect it."

She smiled, thinking about how her own life had taken such an unexpected turn this summer. "It certainly does, Gran. It certainly does."

"I told Brent and Jonah to come for a late breakfast this morning. I suggested we might all have breakfast together after the other guests have finished up," Gran announced as Felicity entered the kitchen the next morning.

"That sounds like a good idea." She couldn't wait to see Brent again. She busied herself at the coffeemaker, hoping Gran wouldn't notice the flush creeping up her neck. Not that they'd have much chance to talk with Jonah and Gran there, but eventually they'd find time. The memory of their almost-kiss from the night before lingered, leaving her wondering when they might pick up where they left off.

Later, Felicity helped Gran clear away the last of the breakfast dishes from the regular guests. As she wiped down the kitchen counter, her stomach fluttered with anticipation. She glanced at the clock for what felt like the hundredth time that morning.

"They'll be here soon enough," Gran said with a knowing smile. "Why don't you get the cinnamon streusel out of the oven? It should be just about done."

Nodding, she slipped on the oven mitts and carefully removed the pan. The warm, spicy scent filled the kitchen, reminding her of cozy mornings from her childhood. She set it on the cooling rack and began slicing it into generous portions.

Gran busied herself arranging a platter of fresh fruit—juicy strawberries, ripe melon chunks, and plump blueberries. "There," Gran said, stepping back to admire her handiwork. "That should do nicely."

Just then, Brent popped his head into the kitchen. "Ready for us?"

Her heart skipped a beat as she smoothed her hair and straightened her apron.

"Come on in," Gran said.

Brent entered first, his eyes finding Felicity's immediately. She felt a blush creep up her cheeks as she once again recalled their near-kiss from the night before. Jonah followed close behind, looking a bit uncertain but offering a friendly smile.

"Good morning," Brent said, his gaze lingering on Felicity. "Something smells amazing in here."

"That would be Felicity's cinnamon streusel," Gran said proudly. "An old family recipe."

They all settled around the table, and she found herself seated next to Brent. As she reached for the coffeepot to pour everyone a cup, her hand brushed against his. The brief contact sent a tingle up her arm.

"This looks wonderful," Jonah said, eyeing the spread before them. "I can't remember the last time I had a home-cooked breakfast like this."

She served up slices of the warm streusel on each of their plates, followed by helpings of fresh fruit. The rich aroma of coffee mingled with the sweet scent of cinnamon as they began to eat.

Brent glanced at her a time or two, as if he knew unanswered questions hung between them. She tried to put them out of her mind and listen to the breakfast conversation.

"So, what do you think of the island now that you've returned?" Gran asked Jonah.

"I didn't see much, but it looks the same. Yet different, I guess. The ferry landing is completely different."

"Yes, it was damaged a few times in the storms that came through. And the lighthouse looks different now. It's been rebuilt. You should go see it."

"I will."

"So, do you two have any plans for today?" Gran eyed Brent and Jonah.

"I'm not sure." Brent turned to Jonah. "What would you like to do?"

"I have a suggestion." Gran put down her fork and looked directly at Jonah. "I think Jonah should go visit Eleanor."

"I'm not sure she'd want to see me after all this time. She's had her own life to live. One she chose." Jonah's eyes held sadness in their depths.

"Ah, Jonah. Don't be foolish. I could always see by the way she looked at you that she cared deeply for you." Gran shook her head. "You two didn't have a chance back then. Not against the wishes of her father and her family. But now… why not go visit her and… Well, see what happens."

"I'm not sure that's a good idea."

Gran shook her head. "I think it's a marvelous idea."

Felicity looked over at Jonah. Didn't he realize there was no use arguing with Gran when Gran had her mind set?

CHAPTER 24

Jonah argued with himself all morning about whether he should go over to see Eleanor or not. But, in the end, he knew there was no way he could *not* go see her. He had to. Even if it was just one last time. See her face. Her smile. Hear her voice.

Jonah walked down the familiar, and yet not so familiar, streets of Magnolia Key, his heart pounding with each step that brought him closer to Ellie's house. The years had passed, but the island remained largely unchanged, as if time had stood still during his absence. The sunlit sidewalks and quaint cottages brought back memories of a life he had left behind, a life that had once included Ellie.

As he approached her house, his thoughts

rambled with questions and uncertainties. What would Ellie be like now, after all these years? Would she still possess the same spirit and warm smile that had captured his heart so long ago? Most importantly, would she find it in her heart to forgive him for allowing her to believe he had perished in the hurricane?

His steps slowed as he neared the white picket fence surrounding Ellie's yard. He caught a glimpse of her, kneeling among the vibrant blooms of her flower garden. Her silver hair was tucked beneath a floppy-brimmed hat, shielding her face from the sun's rays. Beside her, an old Cavalier King Charles Spaniel lay in the shade, its tail thumping lazily against the ground.

Taking a deep breath, he unlatched the gate and stepped into the yard. The sound of his footsteps on the path alerted Ellie to his presence, and she looked up from her gardening. As their eyes met, Jonah felt a rush of emotions—love, regret, and a desperate hope for understanding.

Ellie slowly rose to her feet, removing her hat as she took in the sight of him. Her eyes widened in disbelief, and her lips parted as if to speak, but no words came. He moved closer, reaching out to steady her, and stood before her, his heart laid bare, waiting for her reaction.

"Ellie…" he began, his voice barely above a whisper. "It's me, Jonah."

She pulled off her gardening gloves, letting them drop to the ground. Her hand trembled as she reached out to touch his face, her fingertips grazing his weathered skin. "Jonah? Is it really you?" Her voice quivered with a mixture of shock and wonder.

He nodded, covering her hand with his own. "Yes, Ellie. It's really me. I'm so sorry for… for everything."

Tears welled up in her eyes as she struggled to comprehend the reality of his presence. "But… how? We thought you were… We had a memorial service for you."

"I know, and I'm sorry for the pain I caused you. I had my reasons for staying away, but I never stopped loving you, Ellie. Not for a single day."

Her tears spilled over, trailing down her cheeks. "Oh, Jonah… I have so many questions. So much time has passed."

He gently wiped away her tears with his thumb. "I know, and I promise to tell you everything. But for now, can you find it in your heart to forgive an old fool who made a terrible mistake?"

She looked into his eyes, searching for the truth behind his words. After a moment, she nodded, a tentative smile gracing her lips. "I do, Jonah. I forgive you." She poked her finger at his chest. "But you have a lot of explaining to do."

Jonah chuckled softly, relief washing over him. "I know, and I will. I promise."

Eleanor tried to collect her wits about her. Jonah. After all these years. And he was alive. *Alive.* Her heart thundered in her chest, and if she wouldn't have looked like an old fool, she would have pinched herself to make sure she wasn't dreaming. Instead, she just said, "Let's go in. I have some freshly made sweet tea." She said it as if it was the most normal thing to be inviting Jonah Burton into her home.

"Come on, Winston. Let's go in.'"

She led Jonah and Winston into the sitting room, her mind reeling with the shock of seeing him alive after all these years. She excused herself to the kitchen, needing a moment to compose herself as she prepared a tray of sweet tea.

With shaking hands, she placed the glasses on the tray, the ice clinking against the sides. How many times had she imagined what she would say to Jonah if she ever saw him again, never thinking it was truly possible? And now, here he was, standing in her home as if no time had passed at all.

She carried the tray back to the sitting room, where Jonah stood by the window, his gaze fixed on the view outside. Winston settled onto his bed in the corner, seemingly unperturbed by the unexpected visitor.

"I never would have been invited into your home back then," Jonah said, his voice tinged with a hint of bitterness.

She set the tray down on the coffee table, the memory of their shared past hanging heavy in the air. "No, you wouldn't have," she agreed. "Father would never have allowed it."

She sank onto the sofa, her legs suddenly feeling weak beneath her. Jonah turned from the window, his eyes meeting hers. In that moment, it was as if the years melted away and they were young again, their love forbidden by the rigid expectations of her family and society.

"I'm sorry," Jonah said, his voice rough with emotion. "For leaving the way I did. For letting you believe I was dead. But I thought... I thought it would be easier for you. Easier for you to marry Theodore."

"And all these years, I thought it was my fault you died. You were at the docks because I was supposed to come meet you. But I never showed up. And then... you were gone. I blamed myself."

"Oh, I'm so sorry Ellie. It wasn't your fault. I understood when you didn't show up that you chose Theodore. I didn't blame you for making that choice, but it hurt deeply. It was easier to just go away. I couldn't bear to see you with him."

"I was a young fool." She shook her head, tears pricking at the corners of her eyes. "I guess you did what you had to do. We both did."

He crossed the room and sat down beside her, his presence both familiar and strange. "I never stopped thinking about you, Ellie. Not for a single day."

The use of her old nickname, the one only he had ever called her, made her heart ache with longing. She reached out and took his hand, marveling at the way it still fit perfectly in hers.

"I never stopped loving you," she whispered, the words tumbling out before she could stop them.

His eyes widened, and for a moment, she feared she had said too much. But then he smiled, a soft, gentle smile that made her feel like everything might be all right after all.

"I never stopped loving you either," he said, his thumb stroking the back of her hand.

They sat like that for a long time, their hands intertwined, as the years of separation melted away. There was still so much to say, so much to discuss, but for now, it was enough to simply be in each other's presence, to know that the love they had once shared had never truly died.

Eleanor sat up late that night, sleep eluding her. Winston had long abandoned her and was snoring softly in his bed. She got up from her dressing table and walked over to the window, looking out over her garden softly lit by the light of the moon.

Her choice all those years ago had shaped her destiny. Shaped Jonah's destiny.

Choices always have consequences.

Like her choice to marry Theodore. Like the choices Vera had made to be with Lawrence. And Lawrence's feelings for Vera. And suddenly, she realized that Lawrence was just like her. He'd married who he was expected to marry, who his family wanted him to marry, instead of the woman he loved.

Eleanor let out a long, deep sigh. She should have stood up to her father all those years ago. Gone to meet Jonah that night. All these years she'd blamed herself for Jonah's death. Because if she'd gone to meet him, he would have been with her instead of working on the docks, securing the boats.

And yet, here she was, with the unexpected gift that Jonah was still alive. And the pain that tore at her for all of her adult life was eased with the knowledge he lived. Her choice hadn't killed him.

She walked back and forth in the room, restless. If only she'd chosen Jonah all those years ago. Her life would have been so different. She wouldn't have been trapped in a loveless marriage... albeit one of her own choosing.

And maybe her children would have had a lick of sense, unlike Cliff and his ridiculous idea to put up a high-rise on the island.

Life had a funny way of pointing out your mistakes, and she'd made many. She sat back down at her dressing table and pulled out the envelope with Jonah's photo in it. She smiled as she ran her finger over it. He'd changed so much, and yet not a bit. Some grey threaded through his dark brown hair. His face was weathered from years of working outdoors. But his smile… it was still the same. And the way he looked at her? Yes, that was still the same too.

She set the photo out, resting against the mirror, no longer hidden away in the drawer.

CHAPTER 25

The next morning after breakfast, Felicity went for a walk on the beach with Brent. Gran had practically thrown them out of the house and insisted they go off alone. Which was fine with Felicity, because she couldn't wait to have a chance to talk with Brent again. Something or someone kept interrupting them.

Her bare feet sank into the warm sand as she strolled along the beach with Brent, his hand strong and reassuring in hers. She found herself stealing glances at him as they walked. The morning sun sparkled across the water, and a gentle breeze carried the salty scent of the ocean.

"I can't believe how much has changed in

just a few weeks," she said, breaking the comfortable silence between them.

He squeezed her hand. "Good changes, I hope?"

She stopped and nodded. "Definitely good. I feel like I'm rediscovering myself here on Magnolia Key. I have no desire to leave. Ever."

"Ever?"

"There is just something that Magnolia brings to me. A part of me that's been missing. I'll sort out what I'm going to do here, but in the meantime, Gran can use my help at the B&B." She turned to him. "And what are your plans? I mean, after you finish your research."

"Well, for now, I can find no definitive proof about anything actually going on between Vera and Lawrence. We know he had feelings for her, but since the letter was still in the wall at the B&B, Vera never got it. I guess he never acted on his feelings. And even with my research— and I swear I really did research diligently— Vera just disappeared sometime in the late 1920s or early 1930s. I can't find a trace of her in any records."

"So you're not going to publish anything about them?"

"Not without concrete proof. I don't publish things I can't prove."

"And if someone else discovers these rumors about Vera and Lawrence?" She looked up at him.

"They're rumors, that's all."

"So it looks like Miss Eleanor gets a reprieve from people gossiping about her family."

"It does. Except for… well, there is Jonah. Now that he's back." Brent grinned. "Last I saw him this morning, he was headed back to her house. Said he had something important to discuss with her."

"More important than yesterday when he told her he was alive?" A smile tugged at the corner of her mouth.

"I'm not sure. He didn't say what he wanted to talk about. But I'm fairly certain he still has feelings for her." Brent winked at her. "So, we might have some fresh gossip about Miss Eleanor and Uncle Jonah."

He took her hand again, and as they continued their leisurely pace, the lighthouse came into view in the distance, rising up against the clear blue sky, a symbol of stability amid the ever-changing tides. Just like Magnolia Key was her anchor during the changes in her life.

"Want to head over there?" He gestured toward the lighthouse.

"Sure," They veered away from the water's edge, their joined hands swinging gently between them.

As they approached the base of the lighthouse, Brent slowed his steps. He turned to her.

"This is it," he said softly. "This is where my mother was standing in that old photograph."

She watched as his gaze swept over the scene, taking in every detail. She could almost see him superimposing the image of his young mother onto the view before them.

"It's strange," he continued, his voice filled with wonder. "Standing here, seeing what she saw… It makes her feel closer somehow."

She gave his hand a gentle squeeze. "And now you've found your uncle. Things have really changed for you too."

They stood in silence for a moment, the rhythmic sound of the waves providing a soothing backdrop to their thoughts.

"You know," she said, turning to face him, "I'm glad you came to Magnolia Key. Not just because you've uncovered so much about your family, but because…" She paused, feeling a blush creep up her cheeks.

His eyes met hers, warm and encouraging. "Because?"

"Because I met you," she finished softly.

A smile spread across his face, crinkling the corners of his eyes. He pulled her closer, wrapping his arms around her waist. Her heart raced as she tilted her face up toward his, holding her breath, waiting…

The kiss was soft and gentle at first, a tentative exploration of the feelings that had been building between them. But as he wrapped his arms around her, pulling her closer, the kiss deepened, becoming something more.

When they finally broke apart, she rested her forehead against his. "That was…"

"Amazing," he finished for her, a grin spreading across his face.

She laughed, feeling lighter and happier than she had in years. "It really was." She grinned up at him. "Can I have another one?"

And he willingly obliged.

CHAPTER 26

Eleanor paused, looking up from the task of sweeping the porch. Not that it needed it, but she still had restless energy flowing through her. Ever since Jonah had shown up at her house yesterday.

And there he was again. Walking up her front walkway. She pushed a lock of hair away, tucking it behind her ear, then smoothed her skirt.

"Morning, Ellie," he said as he climbed the stairs. "Hope you don't mind I stopped by."

"Of course not. Come, have a seat." She motioned to one of the chairs lining the shady front porch. Winston got up from where he was resting and padded over, settling at Jonah's feet.

Eleanor sat down beside Jonah, still

marveling that he was here. Alive. Right here with her.

"Ellie, we need to talk."

"Okay." She nodded. Yes, they needed to talk. *She* needed to talk.

Jonah took her hand in his, his touch warm and familiar, stirring up old memories. "Ellie, there's no way after we lost all these years that I'm letting you slip away again. I'm not sure where this will go—you and me—and if you don't want this, speak up now." His words came out in a rush. "Otherwise, unless you say no, I'm moving to the island as soon as I get things wrapped up back home. There's plenty of work for me here. And there's… you."

She swallowed hard, trying to find the right words.

"Just tell me you want me to come back. Choose me this time, Ellie. Choose us."

Tears welled up in her eyes. She'd never thought this moment would come. She'd resigned herself to a life alone, always wondering what could have been. But now, here was Jonah, offering her a second chance.

She reached out and touched his face, so familiar, even after all these years. Now it was her time to speak. "Jonah. I want you to come back."

His face broke into a grin that chased away all the years they'd been apart. "I've been waiting a lifetime to hear those words."

She blinked away the tears and squeezed his hands. "I want you, Jonah Burton. The choice I should have made all those years ago."

"But we have our chance now, don't we?" His eyes searched her face.

"We do," she said as a long-awaited smile, full of promise and hope, lifted the corners of her mouth.

He pulled her to her feet, holding her close. She looked out past his shoulder, out past the magnolia tree, up at the brilliant blue sky, dotted with fluffy clouds. And her heart filled with love. For Jonah. For this beautiful island that had always been her home, but now it felt like it was even more so. This was where she was meant to be. With Jonah. Building a new life together, surrounded by the people and the place that she loved.

I hope you enjoyed reading Bayside Beginnings. But what about Darlene? And don't we want more about Eleanor and Jonah? Try Seaside Sunshine, the next book in the series! And don't worry… Beverly will get her own book too.

As always, thanks for reading my stories. I truly appreciate all my readers.

COMFORT CROSSING ~ THE SERIES

The Shop on Main - Book One

The Memory Box - Book Two

The Christmas Cottage - A Holiday Novella (Book 2.5)

The Letter - Book Three

The Christmas Scarf - A Holiday Novella (Book 3.5)

The Magnolia Cafe - Book Four

The Unexpected Wedding - Book Five

The Wedding in the Grove (crossover short story between series - Josephine and Paul from The Letter.)

LIGHTHOUSE POINT ~ THE SERIES

Wish Upon a Shell - Book One

Wedding on the Beach - Book Two

Love at the Lighthouse - Book Three

Cottage near the Point - Book Four

Return to the Island - Book Five

Bungalow by the Bay - Book Six

Christmas Comes to Lighthouse Point - Book Seven

CHARMING INN ~ Return to Lighthouse Point

One Simple Wish - Book One

Two of a Kind - Book Two

Three Little Things - Book Three

Four Short Weeks - Book Four

Five Years or So - Book Five

Six Hours Away - Book Six

Charming Christmas - Book Seven

SWEET RIVER ~ THE SERIES

A Dream to Believe in - Book One

A Memory to Cherish - Book Two

A Song to Remember - Book Three

A Time to Forgive - Book Four

A Summer of Secrets - Book Five

A Moment in the Moonlight - Book Six

MOONBEAM BAY ~ THE SERIES

The Parker Women - Book One

The Parker Cafe - Book Two

A Heather Parker Original - Book Three

The Parker Family Secret - Book Four

Grace Parker's Peach Pie - Book Five

The Perks of Being a Parker - Book Six

BLUE HERON COTTAGES ~ THE SERIES

Memories of the Beach - Book One

Walks along the Shore - Book Two

Bookshop near the Coast - Book Three

Restaurant on the Wharf - Book Four

Lilacs by the Sea - Book Five

Flower Shop on Magnolia - Book Six

Christmas by the Bay - Book Seven

Sea Glass from the Past - Book Eight

MAGNOLIA KEY ~ THE SERIES

Saltwater Sunrise - Book One

Encore Echoes - Book Two

Coastal Candlelight - Book Three

Tidal Treasures - Book Four

Bayside Beginnings - Book Five

And more to come!

CHRISTMAS SEASHELLS AND SNOWFLAKES

Seaside Christmas Wishes

WIND CHIME BEACH ~ A stand-alone novel

INDIGO BAY ~

Sweet Days by the Bay - Kay's complete collection of stories in the Indigo Bay series

ABOUT THE AUTHOR

Kay Correll is a USA Today bestselling author of sweet, heartwarming stories that are a cross between women's fiction and contemporary romance. She is known for her charming small towns, quirky townsfolk, and the enduring strong friendships between the women in her books.

Kay splits her time between the southwest coast of Florida and the Midwest of the U.S. and can often be found out and about with her camera, taking a myriad of photographs, often incorporating them into her book covers. When not lost in her writing or photography, she can be found spending time with her ever-supportive husband, knitting, or playing with her puppies - a cavalier who is too cute for his own good and a naughty but adorable Australian shepherd. Their five boys are all grown now and while she misses the rowdy boy-noise chaos, she is thoroughly enjoying her empty nest years.

Learn more about Kay and her books at kaycorrell.com

While you're there, sign up for her newsletter to hear about new releases, sales, and giveaways.

WHERE TO FIND ME:
My shop: shop.kaycorrell.com
My author website: kaycorrell.com
authorcontact@kaycorrell.com

Join my Facebook Reader Group. We have lots of fun and you'll hear about sales and new releases first!
www.facebook.com/groups/KayCorrell/

I love to hear from my readers. Feel free to contact me at authorcontact@kaycorrell.com

facebook.com/KayCorrellAuthor

instagram.com/kaycorrell

pinterest.com/kaycorrellauthor

amazon.com/author/kaycorrell

bookbub.com/authors/kay-correll